Something's after Jiggy McCue. . . .

Up in my room we waited for the best part of an hour for something to happen. Then Pete said: "I think you dreamed it."

"If I'd dreamed it," I snapped, "Mom and Dad wouldn't have been so uptight, and I'd still have floor-to-ceiling rocking horses and a light."

"Hmm," said Angie Mint. "If you didn't dream it or imagine it, if it all really happened the way you said it did, it sounds like you've got yourself a poltergeist."

Pete smirked. "Poltergeist? As in ghost?"

"What sort of things do they do?" I asked her.

"Oh, silly things. Childish things, like . . ." She looked around for an example and fixed on the framed poster of some dolphins that Mom had hung above my bed because she likes dolphins. "Like making pictures fall off walls."

The picture fell off the wall.

———

Check out two more hilarious adventures starring Jiggy McCue—*The Killer Underpants* and *The Toilet of Doom*.

OTHER PUFFIN BOOKS YOU MAY ENJOY

The BFG   Roald Dahl

Charlie and the Chocolate Factory   Roald Dahl

Horace Splattly: The Cupcaked Crusader   Lawrence David

Horace Splattly: When Second Graders Attack   Lawrence David

The Original Adventures of Hank the Cowdog   John R. Erickson

Summer Reading Is Killing Me!   Jon Scieszka

Tut, Tut   Jon Scieszka

A JIGGY MCCUE
STORY

THE POLTERGOOSE

by MICHAEL LAWRENCE

PUFFIN BOOKS

PUFFIN BOOKS
Published by the Penguin Group
Penguin Putnam Books for Young Readers,
345 Hudson Street, New York, New York 10014, U.S.A.
Penguin Books Ltd, 80 Strand, London WC2R ORL, England
Penguin Books Australia Ltd, 250 Camberwell Road, Camberwell, Victoria 3124, Australia
Penguin Books Canada Ltd, 10 Alcorn Avenue, Toronto, Ontario, Canada M4V 3B2
Penguin Books (N.Z.) Ltd, 182-190 Wairau Road, Auckland 10, New Zealand

Penguin Books Ltd, Registered Offices: Harmondsworth, Middlesex, England

First published in the United States of America by Dutton Children's Books,
a division of Penguin Putnam Books for Young Readers, 2002
Published by Puffin Books,
a division of Penguin Putnam Books for Young Readers, 2003
Originally published in Great Britain by Orchard Books, London, 1999

1 3 5 7 9 10 8 6 4 2

CIP Data is available upon request from the Library of Congress.

Puffin Books ISBN 0-14-250016-X

Printed in the United States of America

For David Joby and Adrian Hayes,

old playmates and school friends,

good kids

THE POLTERGOOSE

1

Listen, let's not waste any time here. Let's get straight to it. This story is about a dead goose. A dead goose that came back to haunt me. Crazy? You bet. But what can I say? It happened. It happened to me, Jiggy McCue. And my friends Pete Garrett and Angie Mint were witnesses.

An unlikely combination, you might think—two boys and a girl. But Pete and Angie and me, we've known one another since we were just bumps pushing our mothers' clothing out of shape. Best pals, that's us, chums, buds to the last gasp. The Three Musketeers, we call ourselves, even if one of us is a woman. "One for all, and all for lunch," we always say. I don't know why.

Now you're probably not wondering why I'm called Jiggy, but I'll tell you anyway. It's because I jig around a lot. Always have. It can come over me anytime and there's nothing I can do about it. The Golden Oldies used to think there was something wrong with my nerves. Not so, my nerves are great. They just like to move around a little. I'm probably the only kid whose room you could go into in the middle of the night and find him doing the cha-cha in his sleep. Mostly, though, I jig when I'm excited or nervous, or when I get agitated—like the day my parents told me we were moving from Borderline Way.

It was all Dad's fault. If he hadn't gone and gotten himself a job at last we'd still have been in the old place and I wouldn't have gotten myself haunted. My father had been out of work for about five years. He said it was because he knew his worth and wouldn't take just anything. Mom said it was because he's useless.

Anyway, Dad got this job (don't ask me what, it's too boring) and to celebrate he went out and got a new old car to replace the fourteen-year-old heap we used to push around town instead of drive. The new one was only five years old, sort of sky blue with silver bits that hardly rattled at all, and you didn't have to kick little heaps of rust into the gutter every time you slammed the door, which was nice.

The only trouble with the new car was that it looked all wrong on the curb outside our cruddy old house.

Some of the neighbors seemed to think so too, and when Dad had replaced the hubcaps and windshield wipers for the third time, and sprayed over the words *Rich jerk* in a slightly different blue, he and Mom started talking about a new house to go with the car while it was still in one piece.

So they bought a house on the Brook Farm Estate. The house where all my troubles started.

2

The Brook Farm Estate is called the Brook Farm Estate because it's built on the place where Brook Farm used to be. Clever, eh? There's no sign of the farm now—it's all bright new houses with half-finished yards, but back when it was still a farm Pete and Angie and I used to do odd jobs there during summer vacation—collecting eggs, raking up cow muck, all the usual barmy farmy stuff. The farmer, Mr. Brook, old Brooky, he didn't pay much and he didn't like kids much, but we sort of liked going there because it was so open and all, and there weren't trash cans and walls with bad wallpaper wherever you looked.

But then the miserable old devil spoiled everything. He retired. Sold the farm to a building firm and this new estate and shopping center started to go up. When we moved in only about half the houses were built and the roads were still being laid and nothing much had been vandalized yet and it felt all wrong. The new house was a palace compared to the old one, but I didn't like it at first. Didn't really want to like it. Pete and Angie still came over, but it wasn't like the old days when they just wandered through the hole in the fence when they felt like it. They thought the new place was cool. Envied me, they said.

"Yeah, but it's not like *home,* is it?" I said.

"That's what's so good about it," said Ange.

We'd been in the new house about three weeks when Mom and Dad decided it should have a name. I wasn't happy about this. We'd always been able to find our house on Borderline Way without calling its name. I said so.

"The house on Borderline Way was just the place we lived in," Mom replied. "This one's special. It deserves a name."

"I like the number," I said. "I think it's a terrific number."

"What's so terrific about twenty-three?" Dad said.

"I don't know, it just . . . has something."

"We'll still keep the number," Mom said. "But a name will give the place an identity. Set it apart from all the others."

"We each put half a dozen names in the hat," Dad said. He shook his dead father's baseball cap under my nose. "Thought we'd see what came up. Let fate decide."

"Fate?" I cried. "Fate? Have you any idea what fate can *do* to people?"

They just grinned, and suddenly I was very nervous. That hat could be stuffed with the kind of names I'd never live down. I leaned against something to stop my knees from shaking. I think it was Stallone, our cat, because something scratched my behind, and it wasn't me.

"Tell you what," Mom said, "to make it fair, why don't you put some names in too?"

Now this was a surprise. "You'd trust me to name our house?"

"'Course we would," Mom said. "Wouldn't we, Mel?"

Blind panic stamped itself on Dad's face for a minute, but then he took a deep breath, cleared his throat, said, "'Course we would," and reached for Mom's hand to give it a little squeeze. He'd been doing that a lot since we moved and it was starting to make me twitch.

"And whichever one comes out is the one we use?" I said. "Even if it's my choice?"

"Of course!" They chortled like a pair of happy maniacs.

"All right then." I reached for a pad and wrote down

six names, right off the top of my head. They were going to regret this.

I folded my bits of paper and dropped them in the ancient baseball cap. Dad shook them all up, and Mom said: "Who's going to choose?"

"It shouldn't be one of us," I said. "We don't want to get the blame."

"Well, there's no one else," Dad said.

"There's no rush. Why don't we just wait till someone knocks on the door? They can pick it out for us."

There was a knock on the door.

"Bingo!" Dad yelled.

It was Pete and Angie. I could have killed them.

We told them about the house name deal and they said cool and I said you're out of your minds, and they tossed for it to decide which of them was going to be the one to ruin my life. Pete won, and he gave me the evil eye as he stuck his mitt in the hat.

I suppose I shouldn't complain. At least the name that came out was one of mine. But when Pete read it out I said, "No, no, do it again. That one was meant as a joke."

"No, Jig," Dad said. "We made an agreement. Whatever came out of that hat was the one we'd use." He smirked at Mom, who smirked back. "*The Dorks* it is then—agreed?"

3

My parents are aliens. They're from another planet. Got to be. I mean, normal people, human beings from planet Earth, they'd say, "Yeah, real scream, kid," and change the subject till everyone forgot about house names. But not them. Oh no. They go right out and pay somebody to paint *The Dorks* on a piece of wood with flowers around it, then screw it to the wall by the front door for all the world to point at and tell their friends. Sometimes, after the sign went up, there'd be someone on the step trying to sell us something we didn't want, like encyclopedias or religion, and you could see it was all they could do to keep from sinking to their knees with a hankie in their mouth. Embarrassing? I still go out with a blanket over my head.

Apart from the name, it wasn't as bad at *The Dorks* as I thought it would be. For one thing the toilet flushed every time. That made a real change, believe me. And for the first time ever we had a built-in electric stove that didn't blow all the fuses on the street whenever you boiled an egg. We had the same old junk furniture, but at least Dad and I could put our muddy feet up on that.

The most important room in the house, of course, was my bedroom. It wasn't like my comfortable old room at Borderline Way—it was neat, it was clean, even smelled nice, but I soon put that right. It was here, in my new room, that it all started.

The first thing that happened was Roger falling off his hook. Roger's my gorilla. I've had him since I was little when Dad brought him home one Christmas. He'd won him as a consolation prize after losing his shirt at an arcade on the way home. (Dad won Roger, I mean, not the other way around.) Roger has these long thin arms and these palms that stick together when they touch. What you do is you loop his arms around something and join his hands so that he hangs from whatever it is. Like a big plastic hook.

Well, there's Roger hanging from the big plastic hook I've fixed to my wall and there's me sitting on my bed daydreaming about putting chewing gum on my most hated teacher's chair or something, and I must have been vaguely looking in Roger's direction because when his hands suddenly flew apart and he fell to the floor, I jumped so high my head almost cracked the ceiling.

"You stupid gorilla!" I yelled, storming over. "You almost gave me a heart attack!" Roger didn't reply. I picked him up. "Nothing to say for yourself, eh?" I hammered his head against the wall a few times. "One more trick like that and you're a rug!"

As I was fixing his hands together again—behind his back as a punishment—there was this crash. I spun around but I was too late to see it, so I could only guess what happened. My guess was this: my pillow, which I'd been leaning on a second before, had lifted off the bed, flown across the room, and slammed into my toy-rocking-horse shelf.

I'll tell you about my toy rocking horses. Mom had been collecting them for me since before I was born. I had about sixty by this time, all sizes, all facing the same way like an army of rocking-horse impressionists looking for a life. Some of them were made of plastic, some of china, some of wood. Every birthday, every Christmas, every excuse, my collection was added to. Not only did I always know I was going to get another one (sometimes a whole family of them), but I could tell they were rocking horses even before I unwrapped them. It wasn't difficult. Wrapping paper does not a disguise make, not for rocking horses.

"Wow, thanks, Mom," I'd say, all bright-eyed with surprise and gratitude. "Thanks, Dad."

"Don't thank me," Dad would mutter. "Last thing I'd give you is another stupid rocking horse."

This was the lifetime's collection of unwanted rocking horses that my pillow flew at and scattered all by itself. All I could do was stand there gulping silently. My mother was just along the landing, dusting something. She heard the crash, stuck her head around the door just in time to stop my silent gulping from becoming a hobby.

"Jiggy, what on earth was . . . ?" Then she saw. "Oh!" She came in, fell to her knees, stared about her at the Great Rocking-Horse Disaster.

"Oh, Jiggy," she said, and "Oh, Jiggy" and "Oh, Jiggy, Jiggy, Jiggy," until finally I remembered my name.

"Don't blame me," were my first words after my hair stopped standing on end. "It was my pillow, it just sort of . . . knocked them down."

Mom glared up at me. "Oh. I see. Your pillow. And you didn't happen to be swinging it around the room at the time, I suppose."

Now this got to me. I mean, I could see the way it looked, but I don't like being accused of things I haven't done.

"If you must know," I said, "I was over there banging Roger's head against the wall. If that makes the walls vibrate and sends pillows and rocking horses flying, well all I can say is this is a pretty feeble excuse for a house we have here."

"Oh look," she said, obviously not hanging on every word, "two of the most delicate ones are . . ." She reached for a couple of glass twins. Ex-glass twins. Now they were glass quads. "These were my favorites," she wailed. "Jiggy, how could you, how *could* you?"

I felt myself go hot under the collar. What do you have to do to get through to some people?

"I'll say it again," I said. "I did not do this. Do you want captions for the hard-of-hearing? Do I have to get someone to stand at the side of the room speaking in sign language? Look. Read my lips. I—am—not—guilty!"

Bad move. The old girl went red in the face. Bug-eyed.

"Don't you *dare* talk to me like that, young man!"

But I was up and running now. Mouth open and flapping.

"I mean, yeah, right, sometimes I want to jump on

rocking horses till they rock no more. Some mornings I have this fierce desire to throw the whole horsey bunch out the window and watch traffic drive over them till lunchtime. *But I am not the Brook Farm Rocking-Horse Killer!*"

Somewhere in all this a big change came over her. She went all sort of saggy and sad. Her forehead became one big crease and her mouth went down at the corners. Suddenly my thirty-seven-year-old mother was a hundred and five.

"I thought you liked them," she said in this little disappointed voice that grabs your heart and wrings it out like a wet sock. "I really thought you liked them."

Then she jumped up and ran out of the room with her knuckles in her mouth.

I felt bad. So bad I forgot to be miffed that she didn't believe me. It must have hurt, hearing my real feelings about the rocking horses after all this time. I should have told her years ago. Right at the start. My first words shouldn't have been "Ma-ma, Da-da." They should have been "No lousy rocking horses!" Then there'd have been none of this.

When I got home from school the next day all the rocking horses had disappeared. In their place was this bowl of white plastic flowers that a hand grenade couldn't destroy. That made me feel even worse. What had she done with the rocking horses? I couldn't ask. And you know, I sort of missed them now they weren't there anymore. I'd grown up with them after all, they'd rocked with me from the cradle, always been there whether I wanted them or not.

It was three days after the rocking-horse incident that the next thing happened.

I was in bed reading a horror story under the comforter by flashlight (the only way to read them) when suddenly . . .

Picture the scene. I'd just gotten to the part where the two kids—Sam and Rod—are pushing back the front door of this dark old house on the hill. They're looking for their mysteriously missing friends and, naturally, there's this storm going like crazy—thunder, lightning, high winds, the works. Well, Sam and Rod, push open the creaking door, and there they are in this massive old dark old hall, which is very, very, *very* eerie. Suddenly the door slams behind them and the bolts are drawn across by this invisible hand, and there's this terrifying wailing sound, and then . . .

And then the comforter lifts off me, floats up to the ceiling, and winds itself around the Chinese paper lamp shade.

"AAAAAARRRRRGGGH!" I said, or something quite like it.

While this was still bouncing around the walls collecting an echo, I heard Mom and Dad come running from different directions, Dad taking the stairs four at a time, Mom shooting out of the bathroom. They were still on their way when the comforter yanked at the lamp shade like it had a life of its own—yanked so hard there was a flash and the light came down, shade, bulb, and all. I stared at the twitching wires in the ceiling and the burst comforter floating carpetward accompanied by white feathers. The comforter came to rest on the floor a split second before the Golden Oldies fell in, all wild-eyed and vocal.

Naturally, the first thing they did was flick the light switch up and down a few thousand times, *click-click, click-click, click-click,* before realizing it was kaput. Silhouetted dramatically in the landing light, they took in the dangling wires. From the dangling wires they looked at me with the pillow in my teeth. Then back at the ceiling. Then back at me. A passing stranger would have thought they were into vertical tennis.

I jumped off the bed and ran to them. There are times in a kid's life when he has to make use of his parents or they might as well not be there. I'd almost reached Mom when I realized that she'd just jumped out of the shower and into a towel. My heels burned two identical grooves in the carpet and I threw myself at Dad instead. And you know what my loving father did? He pushed me away, held me at arm's length by the shoulders, saying heavy, manful things like: "Jiggy, what is all this?" and "What have you been up to here?" and "What happened to the *light?*" Questions, questions, when all I wanted was a decent hug and someone to say, "There, there, son, it's all right, you put your thumb in your mouth and I'll make you some hot chocolate and read you the Barney book I've been saving for emergencies like this."

Once I'd calmed down I explained what had happened, but I needn't have bothered. They thought I'd yanked the light down myself. And when they saw my horror novel they looked at each other, sighed, and confiscated it. Then they left, muttering stuff about not knowing what had gotten into me lately. And me? Did they give any thought to me? Did it so much as tiptoe across their tiny minds that I might be upset about something? What do you think? I was left sitting there all alone on the side of the bed, shaking, waiting for the comforter on the floor to move again. It didn't, and eventually I felt safe enough to crawl under the bed and attempt a bit of shut-eye, cuddling my slippers.

I didn't make it to dreamland. A sort of hiss jerked my eyelids back. I peered out from under the bed. The door was still open, and the landing light was still on, which meant I could just make out the feathers from the comforter doing a little dance in midair. This time I didn't yell. I was all out of yell. I shot out from under the bed, threw myself across the room and along the landing, straight into Mom and Dad's room. Dad was just getting into his pajamas, and I gave him such a shock that he fell on the bed with his bare butt in the air.

"Dad! You've got to see this!"

"Oh, give it a *rest,* Jiggy!" he said, trying to recover his dignity.

"Go back to bed, darling," Mom said. "Enough's enough now."

And that was it. I know them when they're in that sort of mood. Nothing will make them listen. So I gave up. Went downstairs. Spent the rest of the night scrunched up on the couch, shivering. I kept the light on. Didn't sleep a wink.

I hadn't told Pete and Angie about the Great Rocking-Horse Massacre. I thought they might have a bit of a problem with it. "Hey, you two, guess what happened to me last night, there I am sitting in my room minding my own business and my pillow throws itself at my rocking horses, whaddayasay to *that*?" What they'd have said to that was, "Yeah, Jig, fascinating, out of this world, come with us, they say the new doctor down at the clinic's a whiz with raving lunatics."

But now too much was happening to keep it all to myself. I had to share it with someone, and they were my best friends, so I told them—about the rocking horses, the comforter snatching the light, the dancing feathers—and *of course* they twirled their fingers at their temples. So I said, "Okay, come to my house, I'll show you," which wasn't very bright, seeing as there didn't seem to be a pattern to any of this. I mean, like, why should something happen just because I'd organized seating arrangements?

Mom and Dad were both still out at work when we got to my place after school, but Pete and Angie called their folks to let them know where they were. This was a one-call operation. I should mention that although all three of us happen to be from one-child families, Pete and Angie are also from one *parent* families these days. I won't go into what happened to her father and his mother or we'll be here all day, but the thing is that Pete and his dad, Oliver, had just moved in with Angie and her mom, Audrey. To save on the heating bills, Oliver said. They must think we're stupid.

Up in my room we waited for the best part of an hour for something to happen. Then Pete said: "I think you dreamed it."

"If I'd dreamed it," I snapped, "Mom and Dad wouldn't have been so uptight, and I'd still have floor-to-ceiling rocking horses and a light."

Angie looked up at the naked wires. "Is your dad going to fix that?"

"I doubt it," I said. "He doesn't like messing with electricity. Doesn't even change bulbs if he can get someone else to do it."

"So what happens exactly?" Pete said.

"Mom does it. Or I do."

"No, I mean with this stuff flying around."

I slapped my forehead. How many times did I have to go over this? "How many times do I have to go over this?" I said.

"Yeah, well, it seems pretty funny that it only happens when there's nobody around but you."

"I can't help that. I'm just the unhappy victim."

"Hmm," said Angie Mint.

We both looked at her. Her eyes were all screwed up, and she was stroking the beard she didn't have.

"Hmm what?" I said.

"If you didn't dream it or imagine it, if it all really happened the way you say it did, it sounds like you've got yourself a poltergeist."

Pete smirked. "Poltergeist? As in ghost?"

"As in *mischievous* ghost. One that chucks things and makes a general nuisance of itself."

"Sounds like me according to my dad," I said.

"There was this program on TV about them the other night," Angie said.

"I didn't see it," Pete said.

"You were playing your Road Rage computer game."

"What sort of things do they do?" I asked her.

"Oh, silly little things. Childish things, like . . ." She looked around for an example and fixed on the framed poster of some dolphins that Mom had hung above my bed because she likes dolphins. "Like making pictures fall off walls."

The picture fell off the wall.

I peered through the dust kicked up by four Musketeer heels galloping across the room and down the stairs. The front door was still rocking on its hinges as it became clear that this was only the beginning; that "it" had just been waiting to get me alone, and now that we were . . .

For starters, it whipped up the comforter and threw it over me so I had to fight to get out of it, which wasn't very easy. If you want to know the truth, it was like being held in the grip of a . . . well, a comforter. But when I was free, I made a run for it, like Pete and Angie before me, though I didn't make it out of the house the way they did. Farthest I got was the landing, then there was this hiss, followed by this flapping sound, and next thing I know my legs are being attacked by something sharp and pointy and unfriendly. I ran into the bathroom, slammed the door behind me, turned the lock. I was safe. Terrified, speechless, line dancing with the loofah, but safe.

Or so I thought.

SSSSSSssssssssssssssSSSSSSsss

It was in there with me! In the bathroom, jabbing at the toilet seat, lifting it up, letting it fall, lifting it up, letting it—well, you get the idea. I reached behind me to unlock the door just as the hissing, flapping, invisible thing found my dad's talcum powder. Talcum powder that, as usual, Dad hadn't closed right to block off the little holes on top. And now, because of my father's *carelessness,* it was suddenly snowing talc that smelled of "woodspice with extract of birchwood," whatever that is. In seconds the bathroom was covered in the stuff. So was I. I could hardly see for extract of birchwood, let alone woodspice. My only consolation was that I smelled gorgeous.

Half blind, half delirious, half wetting myself, I snatched up the key, found the keyhole, turned the key, flung back the door, and—

SSSSSSssssssssssssssSSSSSSsss

flap-flap-flap-flap-flap-flap

YYYAAAAAAAAAHHHhhhhhhh

The last of these was me going down the banister one-handed, no feet, hissed at and flapped at and pecked at from behind. All this might have been easier to handle if I could have seen what was pecking on me, but I couldn't. Not then. I didn't get to see it till I made it to the living room. I'd just jumped on the couch and was about to plunge my head in one of Mom's big cushions when the talcum-powder snowstorm that had followed me in took on a shape.

The shape of a goose. A big goose. A big *angry* goose.

And then the talc was shooting off in all directions and the goose was trying to get at me through the cushion, and in a jiffy the stuffing was on the outside and I'm standing there with an empty cover. I threw it away, dived under the coffee table—and discovered that it already had a resident, Stallone the cat, scared out of his fur by the thing that was after me. So there I was with my head under a coffee table while an invisible goose remodeled my back end as a strainer and a demented cat tried to scratch my eyes out. It was not a good position to be in.

Then, without warning, all this gratuitous violence stopped. The room went quiet, the goose stopped pecking me, and Stallone slipped away to do what he does best, which is lick like a madman between his hind legs.

My mother had come home.

She entered the room just as I was backing out from under the coffee table. I saw her jaw hit the carpet as she took in a room that had not previously been covered in woodspice with extract of birchwood.

"Jiggy McCue!" she shrieked. "What have you been doing *now*?!"

6

My mother absolutely refused to believe it wasn't me that had covered the house with talcum powder and shredded the cushion—not even when I told her I was being haunted by a goose. Her nose was still a bit in the air the next morning when she handed me the big soft package tied up with a string that arrived just before school, though she hung about to see what it was. It was something I'd have given one of my dad's arms not to receive. A hand-knitted sweater from my grandma.

"It's not my birthday," I said, gaping at it in disbelief.

Mom's eyes had a hard time staying in their sockets too. She tried to focus on the scratchy little note that came with it.

"It says here that even though she never sees you and she may not last much longer, seeing as nobody cares about her, she wants you to know that she's thinking of you." She looked at the sweater again and flinched. "You must write and . . . thank her."

She held it against my chest. It was bright blue with my name on the front. The sweater, not the chest. The letters were luminous orange and as big as a house. My name just hung there, stretching from armpit to armpit like an ax murderer's grin.

"*Thank* her?" I said. "I'm thinking of sending her hate mail."

When I went up to brush my teeth I kicked the sweater under my bed, to fade quietly from living memory. Then I decided to have a stab at getting Dad on my side about the goose and talcum powder thing. You never know with Dad. Sometimes you can get through to him. Not often, because he doesn't usually listen, but sometimes.

He'd gone out to the yard to look at his Rodadoodah bush. Our backyard is sort of L-shaped, and the bottom part is hidden from the house by a high fence. Dad's patch is around there, out of sight. He hates yard work more than anything except cleaning cars and windows, but he'd been going down there to check out the Rodadoodah every hour since the big trip to the garden center the Sunday before. They'd gone there to get things for this rock garden Mom had been planning.

She bought a lot of other stuff besides and planted most of it herself while Dad, worn out from driving ten minutes each way and carrying plants in, got a beer out of the fridge and read the paper. But she deliberately left a couple of things for him. "It's your yard too, Mel," she said. "Perhaps you'd care to plant something . . . ?" Which meant that he'd better if he knew what was good for him.

So Dad read the instructions tied to the leg of the Rodadoodah bush, dug a hole out of sight of the house, and dropped it in. But here's the thing: the following morning it was still alive! He couldn't believe it. Everything he'd ever planted had immediately committed suicide, and here was this Rodadoodah in bloom already. All right, it had been like that when they bought it, but that isn't the point. The point is that the dinky little pink flowers stuck all over it hadn't fallen off when he planted it, and here they were, still in place three days later. It looked as if all he had to do now was pray for rain occasionally.

"Hey, Jig! Am I a gardener or am I a gardener?"

"You ought to be careful," I warned him. "Get it right once and she'll have you out here all the time—even Saturday afternoons."

I saw him go pale. Saturday afternoons were sacred to him. They were football-on-TV times, jump-around-on-the-couch-and-punch-the-air times. "You might have something there," he said, breaking out in a cold sweat.

"Don't worry. If it comes to it, I'll sneak out one night and kill it for you."

He looked relieved. "Thanks, son."

"Dad?" I said. "What would you say if I said I was being haunted by a goose?"

"Is this a riddle?"

"No, straight question."

"I'd probably say you're quackers."

"That's ducks," I said. "This is a goose."

"Oh," he said, and his eyes glazed over. I'd lost him.

7

Before the Golden Oldies bundled me out of Borderline Way against my will, Pete, Angie, and I always walked to school together. But now that I lived on the Brook Farm Estate I had to go from a different direction, so our paths didn't cross. My way took me through the new shopping center. That morning, like every morning, kids were swarming across the square, yelling, kicking squashed cans around, cracking one another on the head with their backpacks, all the usual.

There were some men in the square putting up video cameras, four cameras, one on each side. There'd been so much vandalism in the shopping center since it was finished six months ago that it was already starting to look like it had been brought over by the Vikings. There was this big campaign going on to catch the Brook Farm Vandals, as the local paper called them.

Some people wanted them behind bars; others wanted them sent bungee jumping without a cord. The cameras the men were putting up were pretty big, pretty unmiss-able. Dad said they chose them instead of itty-bitty little spy things because no one in his right mind would vandalize stuff if he *knew* he was being watched.

I met Pete and Angie in our usual corner of the school playground and told them my news.

"A ghost *goose?*" Pete said. "You're pulling my beak."

"It's true, every word. Would I lie to you?"

He pulled open his sleeve and laughed down it. I sighed, and turned to Angie, expecting more of the same. But no, she was looking quite serious—and over her shoulder.

"I believe you," she said. "After yesterday I'd believe you if you said it was a ghost rhinoceros."

"Angie, a picture got fed up with hanging around on a wall," Pete said. "Big deal."

"Big enough to send you flying down the stairs head-first," I reminded him.

"I overreacted." He eyed Angie. "We both did."

But she wasn't having this. "You were sick with terror. You couldn't eat your dinner, you went to bed early with a hot water bottle even though it was a warm night. Mom and Oliver wondered if you were coming down with something."

"What I was coming down with was common sense," Pete said, all superior.

"Ha!" said Angie.

"You don't really believe all this stuff. You can't. Jiggy's putting us on, has to be."

He looked as ruffled as a bad haircut. I don't think he expected Angie to take my side. All our lives we never took sides. We'd always been like that—you know—us against the world, one for all and all for lunch. But now that sides were coming up for grabs, Pete obviously thought Angie would be on his.

"If Jiggy says there's a ghost goose in his house," Angie said, "there's a ghost goose in his house."

I tell you, if she hadn't been one of my best friends, I'd have thrown my arms around her and kissed her.

"You must be going soft," Pete said to her. "Going all *girly* on us all of a sudden."

Angie stiffened. Narrowed her eyes. She put her nose against his. Grabbed his shirt. "What did you say?"

Pete knew he'd made a mistake. Angie has been a tough cookie since the day she dumped her teething rings.

"Just a figure of speech, Ange. Watch the shirt, huh?"

She put him down. I said to her (just her, Pete could do what he liked), I said: "And I had the weirdest feeling coming to school. Like I was being followed."

"Don't tell me." Pete's smirk was back in place, and it was awfully high on the Punch Me scale. "By a dead goose."

"Well yes, *actually*," I replied.

"Heeeeey, is that the time?" He raised his wrist and looked at the watch he wasn't wearing. "Gotta run. Urgent business in Sane Land."

And he ran off across the playground to kick a ball around with a bunch of lowlifes he would normally swim rivers to avoid.

"Don't mind him," Angie said.

"What about you? How do I know you're not just setting me up for the big put-down?"

Angie looked offended. "Jiggy McCue, how long have we known each other?"

"Since we were no-high," I said.

"So do me the courtesy of believing me when I say I believe *you*, all right? Now. Tell me everything."

I told her everything. About the comforter throwing itself over me, about being chased along the landing and down the stairs, about seeing a goose's outline in woodspice with extract of birchwood, about Mom thinking even *that* mess was my fault.

"And you think it followed you to school?"

"I might have imagined that. It might just be getting to me. I kept thinking I heard this sort of . . . hiss."

"Hiss?"

"Geese do that. Remember old Brooky's goose? Chased us for miles just for setting foot in the yard once."

Angie nodded. "Scary old bird. Brooky called it his guard goose. Didn't need a dog with her around," he said.

SSSSS_{ssssssssssss}SSSSS_{sss}

We clutched at each other and jumped three feet in the air. *"Where did that come from?!"* Angie shrieked as we came down.

Some of the nearest kids were looking at us. Bryan Ryan shouted over. "McCue bothering you, Minty?"

"Get lost, Bry-Ry!" Angie shouted back.

"Yeah, get lost, Bry-Ry," I repeated. Ryan shrugged and turned away.

Angie reached out and patted the air nervously. "Can't feel anything."

"You wouldn't, it's a ghost."

"You said you felt it when it chased you. Your legs, your behind."

"That's true." I started patting the air too.

"Lookit them two," Eejit Atkins said a little way off. "Whacha doin', pr'tendin' t' be blind or sumthin'?"

"No," I said, "we're pretending to be stupid. We're doing Eejit Atkins impressions."

"You wanna watch it, McCue," he said, and walked off with his idiot buds, dragging his knuckles on the asphalt.

The bell rang. The bell rang and there was this startled flurrying noise close by.

"What was that?" Angie said.

"The bell," I said.

"No, the sound like flapping wings."

"Wings flapping," I said.

"What say we get outta here?"

"I say terrific," I said as my feet hit the playground at speed.

Angie was at my side as we pushed through others less anxious to get to class. Then there were shouts, panicky shouts, some way behind us as we made it to the main building.

The goose, the ghost goose, flapping and hissing its way through the crowd, was coming after us.

Face-Ache Dakin, our homeroom teacher, isn't exactly what you'd call popular. He picks on you for nothing and is never happier than when he's handing out detentions and stuff. One of the kids who gets the worst treatment from him is his own son, Milo. I suppose he picks on Milo so as not to show favoritism, but on a good day Milo gives as good as he gets, which always goes down well with the class. He did even better than usual the morning Angie and I shook off the ghost goose in the playground. It was just after attendance, and we were getting our things out for one of Face-Ache's boring, boring, *boring* math lessons.

"You, boy, stop talking," growls Dakin.

"I wasn't talking, Dad," replies Milo, then grins at everyone. "Sorry, I mean *sir*."

"One hundred lines by tomorrow morning!"

"What for?" says Milo.

"For answering back."

"Oh, I thought it was for lying—which I wasn't, as you know."

"Careful, mister, or it'll be two hundred."

"Sorry, can't do any lines tonight," Milo says. "Busy, busy."

"What? What did you say?"

"My turn for cooking and cleanup duty." He turns to the class. "Since my mom ran off with a jogger, we take things in turns." He flips back to Daddy. "Macaroni and cheese okay tonight, Pop?"

"Stand up!" screams his doting father in this strangled voice.

"Righto." Milo gets up, hands in pockets.

"And take your hands out of your pockets!"

Milo takes his hands out of his pockets—and gets to work on his nose. I mean, *really* gets to work. I don't know how he does it, probably a bit of string from his pocket, but he tugs this stuff out of one of his nostrils, tugs and tugs until it's about the length of his arm.

The class is having a hard time controlling its joy by this time, but Face-Ache is not so happy. He storms up to Milo's desk and leans over him, neck out like a spring.

"Young man, you will see me after school."

He says this in such a way that you know, you just know, that he's forgotten for a minute that this kid is his own flesh and blood.

Milo hasn't. "I will anyway," he chirps. "I can't avoid you. Unfortunately," he adds, just loud enough for the whole class to catch. By now it's all we can do not to roll in the aisles with our legs in the air.

"Sit down! I will deal with you *later*!"

Milo sits. There's a halo over his head. His father returns to his desk and leans on it with his fists clenched, glowering around at us, daring us to so much as titter behind our hands. He takes several deep slow breaths, then snaps suddenly to attention.

"I shall return in one minute! And I don't want to hear a sound in this room while I'm gone! Not a *murmur,* d'you hear me?"

He attacks the door, flings it back so hard it bounces, then slams it after him, rattling the roof. It's my guess he has to go and do some serious damage to the bike racks, but whatever the reason, his absence gives the class time to collapse in grateful hysteria and give Milo a standing ovation and offers of money to teach us how to do that and get away with it.

It was while Face-Ache was away trying to keep his

head from detonating that an even more memorable kind of hell broke loose.

It started with a hiss.

The first hiss was quieter than the hysterics, and Angie and I were the only ones to hear it, probably because we were half expecting it. Even Pete didn't hear, though he actually sits nearer to me than Angie, right next to me, in fact. In any case, Pete wasn't sitting now, he was standing on his desk making rude signs at the door old Face-Ache had just gone through. But he sure felt it when he got beaked. Another word for that might be goosed, of course, which means that Pete either got beaked by a goose or goosed by a beak, depending on how you look at it.

Anyway, he gave a yell and fell off his desk, and when he got up he was clutching his backside and glaring at me.

"Did you do that?"

I had no intention of answering this. Also, there were other things to think about than Pete's rear end. Like the shouts of terror from across the room as six or seven kids started running around in circles followed by this great flapping noise as the invisible ghost goose chased them, hissing and pecking, pecking and hissing.

Fear spread through the class like wildfire. Before,

there was just the cheerful noise of a roomful of kids celebrating the temporary departure of a teacher they didn't like. Now it was the panic of a roomful of kids being attacked by something big and angry that they couldn't see. I noticed that Pete's mouth had fallen open. It was trying to find words. It found two. They were: "It's true!"

Now in an odd sort of way I felt responsible for all this. For some reason the ghost goose had decided to haunt me, and because it was haunting me it had followed me to school, and because it had followed me to school it was now attacking my classmates. Whether I wanted it or not it was my ghost, and I couldn't just stand there and watch it go after the other kids.

I tore a curtain down from one of the windows. The curtain was orange, but that's probably not important. I stalked the empty space where the goose seemed to be. I tossed the curtain. It fell to the ground, empty. The goose had moved on. Now it was terrorizing another batch.

I changed direction. Around and around the room I went, curtain held out before me, not even sure if you *can* capture a ghost with a curtain, even an orange one. Every time I thought I was close enough to run a test on this, the goose swerved and left me with a curtain full of air. It wasn't hard to tell where it was because that was where things were flying around and kids were reeling and yelling and treading on one another's faces. There was hardly a desk left standing now. Our beloved classroom was rapidly losing popularity as a place to be. Kids were fighting one another to get out the door.

Somewhere in all this I heard Angie's voice. "I'll go and find Face-Ache!" Then Pete's. "I'll come with you! Hang in there, Jig!"

And suddenly the door was closed and the goose and I were alone.

I climbed over a couple of wrecked desks and several chairs, slowly, cautiously. The goose—still hissing and flapping invisibly, but less frantically now—moved ahead of me. It was over by the door now. I got closer. Closer, closer, curtain at the ready.

The door opened.

"Oh no you don't!" I cried, and leaped into action. I threw the curtain, then jumped after it, brought it crashing to the ground, and put all my weight on it. It was moving under me, but it wasn't getting away now.

I'd done it! I'd got it! You *could* catch a ghost!

There was a muffled voice. A muffled angry voice.

Not a goose's voice, which was a bit of a puzzle since it was coming from inside the curtain I was sitting on. It was saying something odd too. Something that sounded awfully like: "McCue, I'm going to have your hide for this!"

I got off the curtain. Looked under it. Face-Ache Dakin glared up at me with eyes like burning coals.

"Sir," I said. "Listen, I can explain everything. . . ."

That night, while Dad hung around on the landing pretending he wasn't there, Mom sat me down quietly on my bed and told me that she was taking me to a behavioral psychologist. "A behavioral psychologist," she told me, "is someone who tries to figure out why a person does the things he does."

I said: "So why don't you take Dad to one?"

"Hey, don't bring me into this," Dad said from the landing, blowing his cover without any trouble.

"Why would I take your father to a behavioral psychologist?"

"The way he carries on when he's watching football?"

"We don't need to take your father anywhere to know why he behaves like that. He behaves like that because he's never grown up."

"Well, neither have I," I said. "And I have an excuse."

But there was nothing I could say. They'd made up their minds. My parents were taking me to a shrink. They were going to have me shrink-wrapped.

Mom kept me home from school the day of the appointment, and we took the bus to town and walked to this old building full of offices where Serious People worked. The door we ended up at had the name Dr. Edward Pickett on it, with all these capital letters after it that didn't make any sense.

We'd been sitting in the waiting room for about fifteen minutes when this tall thin guy appeared, said "Good morning!" in an unnaturally hearty voice, and held open his office door. I took the hint and went in. As the door closed behind me I knew that Mom was already reaching for the first *People* magazine.

It wasn't a very interesting office. It had some shelves with some fat books, and a small neat desk over in one corner with a computer, and there were some filing cabinets and two red leather armchairs facing each other. The walls were covered with these big pointless paintings, all blobs and bits of color that looked like they'd been slapped on with a mop or lobbed with a spoon.

The tall thin guy introduced himself as Dr. Pickett

(surprise, surprise) and pointed to one of the red leather armchairs. This chair was in the middle of the room, while the one he took for himself had its back to the wall, right under the biggest, most pointless painting of all. We both sat down, and I tried not to stare at his hair, which believe me wasn't easy. The doc's hair seemed to end just above his ears, but on one side he had grown it so long it would have touched his shoulder if he'd just let it fall naturally. Instead, he swept it up across his hairless roof, up and over, till it joined the other sad little batch cringing around the opposite ear. He must have oiled this long hair or something because it just lay there on top of his skull, glistening. I wanted to ask him a question. I wanted to say: "Hey, Pickett, explain to me why an expert in the way people behave tries to con us he isn't as bald as a boiled egg." I didn't, of course.

"Make yourself comfortable, er . . . Jiggy," he said, glancing at some notes on a small table beside his chair. I made myself comfortable. "Now I want you to understand that there's nothing to worry about here. We're just going to have a little chat about things. There's nothing to be concerned about."

"I'm not concerned," I said. I didn't tell him that I

was more annoyed than anything. Annoyed that no one believed me when I said I didn't do stuff.

"For someone who's not concerned," the doc said, "you seem to be having some difficulty keeping still."

"Oh, that's just me. I jig around all the time. Always have. That's why I'm called Jiggy."

"Ah."

He raised his hand to his face and spoke into it, so quietly I couldn't hear what he was saying. I felt I shouldn't be listening anyway. This was a personal conversation between him and his hand. While he was talking to his hand my eyes drifted to the picture over his head. It was one of those pictures you couldn't ignore if you wanted to. Pickett caught me looking at this and got kind of excited. It all began to make sense. He sat there under that picture and you sat opposite him, and every time you looked at it because you couldn't ignore it he told his hand about it, and later he played the hand back and decided there was definitely something wrong with you because you kept looking at this pointless picture all the time. This behavioral psycho game, easy money or what?

"Now, Jiggy," he said, removing his hand from his mouth, "I want you to tell me a bit about yourself. Let's start with school, shall we? What do you think about school?"

I didn't want to think anything about school. School and me didn't see eye to eye right now. Not since Face-Ache Dakin hauled me into the principal's office for single-handedly destroying his classroom. Funny, but when it came to it nobody could remember being chased by something noisy, violent, and invisible. All they could remember was me tearing a curtain down and going crazy, jumping over desks and shouting and stuff. Even when Pete and Angie tried to come to my rescue it didn't do any good. Part of the reason for this was that they couldn't quite bring themselves to say that it wasn't me that had made all the mess in the class-room and terrified the kids, but a dead goose. You can see their point.

Dr. Edward Pickett sat there smiling politely while I tried to decide what to tell him about school. The sun-shine was sloping through the window really brightly and hitting the picture over his head so hard it glowed.

"What do I think about school . . . ?" I said thought-fully.

"In your own words," said Pickett.

I was glad he said that. If he hadn't I might have

rushed out into the street and asked a complete stranger what *he* thought of school and rushed right back with the news.

"It's . . . okay," I said.

He leaned forward, obviously fascinated by my opinion on this subject. "Okay?"

I shrugged. "Yeah. Okay."

"You don't mind school?"

I shrugged again. It looked like it would be a shruggy sort of conversation. "Sometimes I can think of other places I'd rather be."

"Such as?"

"Such as the bottom of a coal mine looking for canaries," I said. "Such as on the sole of a hobo's shoe when he's just walked in something a horse dropped. Such as at home, in bed."

"So you don't think much of school?"

"I didn't say that. I said it was okay."

"So you did." He spoke briefly to his hand again. "We might come back to school," he says then, "but let's move on now. Tell me about home. Your home life. For instance, how do you get along with your parents?"

I gave shrug three. "We get along all right."

"Just all right?"

"What do you want, violins and sunsets? They're my parents."

"What I want, Jiggy," Pickett said, like someone trying to talk a cat down from a tree, "is for you to feel free to talk about them any way you please, in your own words."

My own words again. I looked at his hair. Then, so as not to seem rude, I looked at the pointless picture above it. The sun coming through the window was getting brighter by the minute, and the picture was so dazzling now that the colors looked as if they were moving. I was starting to hallucinate.

"My parents are fine. Most of the time."

I had to feed him that last bit. He needed it, I could tell. He had to have something to latch on to.

"Most of the time? Not . . . *all* the time?"

"Do you get along with your parents all the time?" I asked him.

This threw him for a second. "We're not talking about my parents, Jiggy."

"Well look at it from my point of view," I said. "I mean, we're sitting here across from each other, and you, who I never met in my life before, start asking me about my parents. I mean, why should I tell you just because my mom brought me here? I'm not being difficult or anything, it's just that I think this should be a two-way sort of thing, that's all."

He thought about this, then nodded. "Fair comment. But there's nothing I can tell you; my parents are dead."

I wished he had a big goldfish bowl so I could stick my head in it and drown. "Hey," I said, "sorry to hear that. I didn't know or I wouldn't have asked. You miss them?"

"Miss them? Well, yes. Of course. Sometimes. One does."

"Does one?" I said.

"Certainly. One's parents, you know."

"Did you get along with them?"

"We're here to talk about you, Jiggy."

"All I'm asking is did you get along with your parents, like you're asking me, nothing heavy."

He gave this some thought too. He was doing his best to be fair. Or maybe he thought he'd get more out of me if he spilled a couple of beans too.

"As a matter of interest," he said, avoiding my question, "my mother painted the pictures in this room."

I looked around the office. "Yeah? Really?" Now he had me feeling sorry for him. "Including the one behind you?" The sun was so bright on the big picture now that it looked as if it was vibrating. A trick of the light, but it made me nervous.

Pickett glanced up, then back at me. "That's my favorite." He must have seen the pity on my face at that because his lips twitched in this way that says I know about these things and you obviously don't. "I realize they may not be to everyone's taste. Art is such a personal thing."

"You can say that again." Fortunately he didn't.

"Now tell me about your relationship with your parents," he said instead, with a very slight shove on the second "your."

"Put it like this," I said. "I wouldn't necessarily go to the Parent Shop and pick them out as the pair I most want to spend my childhood with, but they could be worse."

Pickett flipped his hand to his mouth, and while he told it about my parents I watched the sun leak out of the big picture and fan out across the top of his head. It was then that I noticed something. Something so attention grabbing that I didn't hear a word of what he said to me next. I hadn't been imagining that the picture over his head was moving. It really was—all of it, not just the painting, the frame too. It was coming away from the wall. Falling. In a few seconds it would be off the wall and on Pickett. Then, about three seconds after I realized this, the sun cast a shadow across the painting.

The shadow of a long thin neck with a small beaked head on top.

I jumped up. Ran across the space between the doc and me yelling something like, "Hey, watch out, watch out!"

I reached up, grabbed the picture by the frame, one hand on each side—but it was too heavy and I was too late! Even with me holding it, it continued on down, and there was this tearing sound, and the next thing I knew I was standing there with the frame in my hands looking down at the top of Pickett's head, which was now poking up through the picture. He sat there staring up at me from the back of his dead mother's painting, his favorite pointless picture. The long strands of hair that he'd so carefully oiled onto his dome had come away. They were hanging down past his ear, past his jaw, his neck, trailing across the back of the canvas resting on his shoulders. And he looked terrified. Of me.

Then he was getting up out of his chair. Stumbling all over the place as he tried to wriggle out of the painting, shouting stuff about me being a delinquent, a vandal, a hopeless case, a . . .

Need I go on?

10

The time had come to take my brain out of its box on top of the dresser, blow the dust off, and put it to work. I told Pete and Angie to bring their brain boxes too, and together we sat down on the floor in my room to think this thing out.

"Something's got to be done," I said. "Something has to be *done*."

"Yeah, but what?" said Pete.

"What we need," said Angie, "is to be logical about this."

"Easy to say when you're talking about being haunted by a dead goose," I chipped in. "I mean, there's logic and logic."

"And dead geese and dead geese," said Pete.

"And this," said Angie, "is no ordinary dead goose. It's a dead goose that breaks things and chases people and pecks them where it hurts. A poltergoose."

I nodded. "That's what we're talking about here, isn't it? A poltergoose."

"Right," said Angie.

"Right," said Pete.

"Question is," I said, "what are we gonna do about it?"

"Yeah," said one of them, or perhaps both. "That's the question."

We put our brains back in the boxes. They hadn't worked.

Silence fell. And stayed fallen for some time, until Pete suddenly said: "Ow!" Then he said it again, with echoes—"Ow-ow-ow-wow-wow-wow!"—and added, "Cramp!" He jumped up, but immediately fell again and lay writhing on the floor, one leg dancing in the air. "Ow-ow-ow-wow-wow-wow!"

"I get that sometimes," Angie said. "Usually first thing in the morning, right after I wake up. It is no fun."

"I don't think I ever had a cramp," I said.

"You're lucky."

"Ow-ow-ow-wow-wow-wow!" said Pete.

"I get stitches, though."

"In your side?" said Ange.

"Yeah. And I don't have to be running or anything."

"Know what you mean. I get them just trying to keep up with Mom in the street. Talk about painful."

"Ow-ow-ow-wow-wow-wow!"

"And pins and needles," I said. "That's almost worse."

"Right. Pins and needles. First time I had them we were visiting this sort of cousin of Mom's, this really boring visit."

"Ow-ow-ow-wow-wow-wow!" said Pete.

"And there's this piano that the sort of cousin is playing really ancient songs on," Angie went on, "and there was nothing else to do but lean on it. The piano."

"Tough," I said.

"Owwwwwwwwwww," said Pete.

"And I'm leaning there, and I get this weird feeling in my elbow that spreads along my whole arm, and I start dancing around, yelling, 'I've broken my arm, I've broken my arm!' and everybody laughs themselves stupid, which didn't help at *all*. I mean, *I* didn't know it wasn't fatal, did I?"

Pete stopped shaking his leg. "Whew," he said. "Next time that happens I'm sawing it off."

I got up. Walked across the room to put some music on. I was flipping through my tapes and CDs when Angie said: "Oh, very funny, Jig. I'm killing myself here."

"Whassat?" I said, without turning around. "I gotta

get some new stuff. There's nothing here under three weeks old."

"How do you do that anyway?" Pete asked. "Clever. Can't see your hands."

"My hands?"

"You've been practicing, haven't you?"

"What are you talking about?" I turned.

They were sitting there on the floor gazing at this stretch of wall that had been blank and would still be blank if it wasn't for the shadow on it. My saliva turned to dust.

"That has nothing to do with me," I said.

Pete and Angie turned to look at me. "You can't fool us."

I watched the goose shadow's eyehole close slowly, then open again. I held my hands out so they could see them. They looked from me back to the wall. The shadow was still there. The beak opened.

"You're . . . not doing that?" Angie said.

SSSSSSssssssssssssSSSSSSSsss

She and Pete got up. Slowly. Backed away from the shadow wall. Slowly. When they reached me, we stood as close together as we could without actually climbing into one another's clothes.

"What now?" one of us said.

"Run," said another.

"Right," said whoever's turn it was next.

We would have too. Except that as we set off at a fast tiptoe around the edge of the room, each trying to put someone else in front and someone else behind, the goose shadow turned its head to follow us.

But then the sun went behind a cloud and the goose faded to nothing. We gave a big gasp of relief. Three gasps. Angie stepped away from the rest of us to investigate the sudden shortage of goose shadow. And lived to regret it.

"YAAAAAAAAAAAAAAAAAAAAAAAH!" she said as she flew across the room.

Angie Mint lay in a crumpled heap on the floor just below the wall she'd almost hit. It could have been nasty. She might have gone just that bit farther and ruined the wallpaper.

"You all right?" I said from where I was.

"Do you mind if I don't answer that?" the crumpled heap replied.

"Cool with me, Ange," I said.

Angie came back across the carpet, on her rear end, a little at a time, as if she was half expecting to be picked

y
60

up and thrown again. When she made it back to us we stood waiting for something else to happen. Nothing did. Even the sun stayed behind its cloud.

"I think we ought to make a move," Pete whispered.

"I just did and look what happened," Angie said.

"Well, I'm not sticking around to be thrown at walls."

"See you then," I said.

"See you." He didn't move.

"Well, go on if you're going," Angie said.

"I will, I will. When I'm ready."

There was a long pause.

"When are you going to be ready?" I asked him.

"When I'm *ready* already, all right?"

An even longer pause. Then he was off, heading for the door. Running. But what a run. A run like no other I ever saw in real life. Not a fast-as-lightning get-me-outta-here type run. No, this was in slow motion, like in an action film.

When he was halfway across the room, running for all he was worth at a hundred feet a month, the door opened. By itself. Pete looked happier about that than he did about running slowly. Door open, that meant he could go. He would be out there on the landing any day now.

And he would have been too, if not for one small detail. The one small detail was that just as he was about half an arm short of it, the door closed again. The door closed, but still Pete went on. He couldn't stop. He was going so fast now he could have almost passed a wounded snail. He reached for the door handle. He turned it. Pulled. The door wouldn't budge.

SSSSSSSssssssssssssSSSSSSSSsss

Pete yelled, clutched the front of his jeans where he'd just been pecked, and bounced back into the room at suddenly normal speed.

Some minutes later, when we were once again sitting on the floor, backs to the wall, Angie said: "You know what I think? I think the goose doesn't actually mean us any harm."

Pete gaped at her in disbelief. "Doesn't mean us any harm? After what it just did to me?"

"That didn't really hurt. It just gave you a little nip, or you wouldn't have any color in your cheeks."

"You know, Ange might have something there," I said. "The goose could have slammed her against the wall but it dropped her short. And you know in class? It only *scared* the kids, nothing else. And when it pecked me down the stairs it didn't really do any damage, just sort of . . . rattled me."

"That's right," Angie said. "I think it's simply trying to make us notice it."

"It succeeded," said Pete.

HONK!

Our heads hit the wall behind us.

"It's still here," I said, in case nobody else had realized.

"And honking," said Angie.

"Old Brooky's goose used to honk like that."

"All geese honk," Pete said.

"You don't think it could *be* old Brooky's goose?" This was Angie.

"Nah. Even geese have to be dead before they can haunt people."

"Has anyone seen Brooky's goose around lately?"

"Well, of course we haven't," I said. "The farm isn't here anymore."

"Probably lives with him in that new bungalow of his," said Pete.

HONK!

"I think we'd better go and find out for sure," said Angie.

HONK! HONK! HONK!

"Definitely," I said.

We slid up the wall, very, very slowly. There was a low hiss from across the room.

"It's all right, goosey." Angie waved her hands at nothing in a calming sort of way. "We're on your side. We're the good guys."

"We are?" Pete said. "I thought we were trying to get rid of it."

HONK! HONK! HONK! HONK! HONK! HONK!

We made a run for it. This time the goose didn't do any haunty sort of tricks like make us go in slow-mo, or open and close the door just as we got to it, or throw us across the room. Maybe it knew it had gotten through to us. Maybe we were onto something here. We threw ourselves down the stairs and out into the street.

The bungalow that Linus Brook had bought with the stash he got for his cruddy old farm was about where his cowshed used to be. Like my brainless parents, Brooky had given his new home a name. The name he gave his bungalow was painted on a piece of black slate beside the plastic doorbell.

LAST STAND

We pressed the plastic bell and waited until the national anthem finished so old Brooky could stop standing at attention on the other side of the glass door and open it.

"Hi, Mr. Brook," I said.

There were huge bags under his eyes and he hadn't shaved for a week. There was no collar on his shirt and not many buttons either. There was dirt beneath his nails, enough hair in his ears to thatch a poodle, and his teeth were yellow, black, or at the dentist's without him.

"Shove off," he snarled. Same lovable old Brooky.

"It's us," I said. "Jiggy, Pete, and Angie from Borderline Way."

"Angie, Pete, and Jiggy," said Angie.

"Pete, Angie, and him," said Pete.

"Never heard of you," said Brooky, and slammed the door.

We looked at one another. Something had gone wrong somewhere. Angie pressed the bell again. Ten minutes later, when the national anthem had died once more, Brooky ripped the door back.

"You remember us," Angie said brightly before he could speak. "We used to help out on the farm during vacations."

"For peanuts," Pete muttered. He never did care for old Brook.

"A lot of kids helped on the farm. If you can call it help. No reason to come bothering me here, I'm retired."

He slammed the door. We stood looking at it, and at him standing behind the glass like a statue, either waiting for us to go or try again.

"This is ridiculous," I said.

"Yep," said Angie.

"Leave it to me," said Pete, and stepped forward. He didn't bother with the bell. He used his fist.

The door opened.

"I s'pose you think you can get a free cup of coffee outta me," Mr. Brook said.

"Only if you're making some," Angie said over Pete's shoulder.

"Making some what?"

"Er—coffee?"

"Why would I make coffee?" he growled. "I hate coffee. I always hated coffee. Coffee is my most hated thing on earth. After kids, that is."

He slammed the door. Once again we stood looking at it. It was a nice enough door, but not so nice we wanted to spend our lives in front of it.

"Was he always like this?" I said.

"Like what?" said Pete.

I punched him on the shoulder. He punched me back. The door flew open. Old Brook grabbed us by the punched shoulders.

"I won't have you young ruffians fighting on my doorstep!" He banged our heads together. "Now clear off before I buy a dog and set it on you."

While Pete and I staggered around, groaning and holding our heads, Angie stepped between us and put a foot in the door that old Brooky was about to slam for the fourth time. Being in pain I wasn't paying much attention, but when Angie said the word "goose" I saw Brooky pass a hand over his eyes and his chest cave in.

"There used to be one around the farmhouse all the time," Angie was saying. "Remember her?"

Brooky let out a tremendous wail and fell facedown on the Welcome mat, sobbing.

Angie dropped to her knees beside him. "Mr. Brook?"

"Aunt Hetty," the old boy said. "Sob, sob, sob. Sob, sob, sob, sob, sob, sob, sob!"

"Aunt Hetty?" Angie said over the sobs. "Is that the name of your goose?"

"Was," he said to the Welcome mat. "Wa-a-a-a-a-a-as."

"Was!" Angie sat back in triumph and beamed up at us. "So she *is* dead! Good news!"

"EEEERRRRAAAAGGGHHH!" wailed Linus Brook, miserable old farmer turned miserable old retired bungalow-dweller.

"Why don't we get him off the mat?" I suggested.

Pete and I got under Brooky's armpits and hauled

him to his feet. Then we half carried, half dragged him into his living room. We were just about to drop him in a chair facing a cold radiator when Angie said: "Look at this."

She'd gone on ahead and was standing by the mantel. We joined her, carting Brooky along with us. She was looking at a framed photo of the goose that had been better than a guard dog.

"Hetty." Brooky reached between us and grabbed the goose photo. A great fat tear squeezed out of his eye, plopped onto the glass. He smeared it away with a thumb.

Then, bit by bit, we got the story. Brooky told us that his wife had never cared for his favorite goose, Aunt Hetty, but when Mrs. Brook died he took Hetty in, gave her the guest room. He called it the Guest Goose Room and decorated it specially, goosey wallpaper, goosey curtains, goose-feather pillows, the works.

"Real company she was. Someone I could really talk to. Never could talk to the wife. All she ever did was sit there knitting and watching TV. But Hetty, she didn't like TV. Didn't seem to see any point in it. And as for knitting . . ."

"What happened to her?" Angie asked, all soft and dewy-eyed.

Brook was now sitting in a chair, the photo of the goose on his lap. "I killed her," he said.

Angie's face turned to stone. Her eyes went as hard as peppermints. Her voice became a foghorn. "YOU KILLED HER? YOU KILLED YOUR *FRIEND*?"

Brooky shook so hard his last few teeth almost popped out. He shrank deep into his cardigan.

"I mean in a manner of *speaking*. I didn't *actually* kill her. Not personally. I wouldn't do a thing like that. If she was still alive I'd have her here with me at *Last Stand*. I . . . I *loved* that goose."

Angie unclenched her fists and took several deep calming breaths and tried to look sympathetic again. "So what happened?"

"I'd just sold the land," Brooky answered, twitching in one damp eye. "The builders were laying the foundations of the new houses, and old Het didn't like all those strangers around the place with their thumping vehicles, their radios and all. Thought they was trespassing. I had to keep her in when the builders were around."

"*And?*" Angie said, just managing not to tap her foot.

"Well, my house was the last thing to go. They had to build this place for me before I'd let 'em knock the house down. But one day Hetty got out. I don't know how. I'd gone into town to cash my pension check. When I got back she was lying there, squashed flat. Dead as a doornail. One of the builders had run over her with his bulldozer."

"Goosedozer," Pete muttered.

"They said it was an accident," Mr. Brook went on, "and maybe it was, but I always had this suspicion that she went after them and they did her in. Saddest day of my life, that was, seeing poor Hetty lying there like that. No more honking, no more hissing, no more knocking the knickknacks over when the national anthem started up."

I leaned closer to him. I had a personal interest in this. "What happened to the body, Mr. Brook?"

"The body?" He looked up at me and gave another of his pathetic little sobs. "It was all I could do to dig the grave. All my fault, see. That's what I meant. I as good as killed her when I sold the farm. If I hadn't sold up she'd still be here today, with me."

"Yes. But where did you bury her?"

"Right where she fell," he said. "I couldn't have carted her off someplace else. I was too upset."

"But where *was* that?" I said through my teeth.

"Where?" He gave this some serious thought. "I don't know," he said at last. "One of the new yards they were laying out, I think."

"I don't suppose it's any good asking you *which* yard?"

He shook his head. "All looked the same to me. Still do." He lifted the goose photo and stared at it, the tears welling up again. "Felt bad about that later on, burying her just anywhere, but it was too late by then, the houses were sold. All private property, and none of it mine." He gave an enormous sigh. "Should have given old Het a decent burial. The wife had one, and I liked Hetty better."

When we left Brooky's there was one big question in our minds: if the poltergoose was Aunt Hetty's restless spirit and her body was buried in one of the new back-yards and the yard happened to be mine, which *part* of the yard was she in? It would have helped if Mr. Brook had left a gravestone or something. Mom could always have grown something against it.

"Yeah, but even if we did find Hetty's body," Pete said as we strolled back to my place, "it wouldn't mean she's the poltergoose, would it? Necessarily."

"Bit of a coincidence if she wasn't," Angie said.

"Maybe. But if we found it and it *was* the polter-goose's, what would we do with it?"

"We'd move it," I said. "Bury it someplace else. If she's somewhere else she might stop haunting me."

"Then she might haunt some*one* else."

"Their problem. Me, I'll be out celebrating."

"Maybe Hetty's haunting you because she *wants* you to move her," Angie said.

"What, to someone else's yard?"

"No, not someone else's yard. Perhaps she wants a decent burial, like old Brooky's wife."

"I don't think they hold funeral services for dead geese," I said.

"I don't mean an actual service. But from what Brooky said he treated her as almost human. So perhaps Aunt Hetty *thought* of herself as human. If she did, naturally she'd want to be laid to rest in a human sort of way."

"You don't mean in a *coffin*?!" Pete said.

"No, I mean just . . . just something better than being dropped in a hole near where she hissed her last."

"Like what?" I said. "Like where?"

"If I was her," Angie said, "I'd want to be put in a place where I'd been happy. Like the farmhouse. I bet she loved it there. Yeah, bury her where the house used to be, and her spirit might find peace and stop bugging people."

"Snag," Pete said.

"There's always a snag with you, isn't there?" I said to him. "What now?"

"You know what they built where Brooky's house was?"

"What?"

"The new shopping center."

12

Back home Mom was out in the backyard working on her rock garden. She'd planted half the planet in it by this time and was as proud of it as Dad was of the Rodadoodah bush still being alive.

"Very nice, Peg," said Pete, the crawler.

Mom looked pleased. "Well, thanks, Pete."

"Are you going to be out here long?" I asked her.

"Why, do you want company while you mow the grass for me?"

"No chance. Yard work's for wimps. Just asking."

"As a matter of fact, I'm going shopping in a minute. Is there anything you want—apart from chips, chocolate, fizzy drinks, and everything else that does you no good at all?"

"No, just those."

We went up to my room. And—

SSSSS ssssssssssssSSSSSS sss

The goose's shadow was waiting for us on the wall. Pete backed into me. "Let's go," he said.

"No," Angie said. "We have to sort this thing out once and for all. And did you notice anything about that hiss? It was almost gentle. As if it's glad to see us."

SSSSS ssssssssssssSSSSSS sss

She was right. Gentle. Definitely gentle. Angie stepped farther into the room.

"Goose," she said boldly to the shadow on the wall. "Goose, are you Aunt Hetty?"

And you know what the goose shadow did? It winked. True as I stand here. Then dipped its neck a couple of times like it was saying "You got it, gal."

"Yes!" I said, punching air.

"I've got an idea." Angie held her arm out so the sun cast a shadow of it on the wall, then opened her hand so its shadow was offering a palm to the goose shadow.

And Aunt Hetty's shadow dipped its beak and touched the shadow of Angie's hand—very gently.

"Hey," Pete said, impressed.

"You feel anything, Ange?" I said.

"Sort of a tickle. I think she wants to be friends."

"Ask her if she's buried in my backyard."

"She might not like to think about where she's buried. She might throw me at the ceiling or something."

"We've got to chance it."

"You mean *I* have to." But she squared up to the goose shadow and cleared her throat. "Aunt Hetty, are you buried in Jiggy's backyard?"

SSSSSSsssssssssssssSSSSSSSsss

"Sounds like a yes," said Pete.

"Ask her if she can show us where exactly," I said.

"Hetty, can you show us exactly where you're buried?"

The goose shadow nodded.

"Ask her if she'd like us to dig her up and bury her somewhere else," I said.

"Would you like us to dig you up and bury you somewhere else?"

SSSSSSsssssssssssssSSSSSSSsss

"Ask her if she wants to be buried where Mr. Brook's old house was."

Angie turned on me. She seemed peeved. "Why am I doing all the asking? Your mouth seized up all of a sudden?"

"You're doing such a great job," I told her.

"Huh!" But she asked. "Hetty, do you want to be buried where the old farmhouse used to be?"

SSSSSSssssssssssssssssSSSSSsss

"That is one clever dead goose," I said admiringly.

"Not necessarily," said Killjoy Pete. "Maybe 'SSSsssss' is the only word she can say."

There was a sudden knock on the door. Have you noticed how knocks on the door are always sudden? Not only in books either.

"Can I come in, kids?"

Silent Panic. If Mom came in she'd see the . . .

We needn't have worried. The shadow of the goose vanished while we blinked.

I opened the door.

"I'm leaving now," Mom said. "Will you be all right here for half an hour?"

"Sure," I said. "Great. Take longer if you want. Take all day. In fact—"

"Half an hour should do. I'm just getting a few things in for the housewarming dinner."

"The what? Oh, that. I thought it was tomorrow."

"It is tomorrow, but I have some things to prepare, and I want it to be really special."

I glanced at Pete and Angie. They glanced back. All our faces said, Saaaaaad. Housewarming dinner. The things Golden Oldies get excited about breaks your heart.

The poor old parent was about to leave us in peace when she remembered something. "Jiggy, I've been meaning to ask. Where did you put that sweater your grandma sent you?"

"Sweater?"

"The one she went to such trouble to knit for you with her own hands? The one with your *name* on it?"

"Oh, that thing. I stuck it under the bed."

"Well, would you kindly *unstick* it and put it in your sweater drawer?" She turned away. I started to close the door. "Oh, and Jiggy."

Angie and Pete and I looked at the ceiling. "Yes, Mother?"

"Try not to turn the house to rubble while I'm gone—please?"

It wasn't till we heard the front door close that Aunt Hetty's shadow came back. Then I said: "Ready, Musketeers?"

Pete and Angie nodded. So did Hetty.

"One for all and all for lunch," three of us said. Hetty just hissed.

We went downstairs. On the way down we could see Hetty's shadow along with ours where patches of sunlight fell on the wall, but once we were out in the yard we couldn't see her at all. It was very bright out there.

"Aunt Hetty?" I said.

SSSSSSsssssssssssssSSSSSSsss

Which, as everybody knows, is Goose for "Yep! Here!"

"Show us where you're buried, Het."

There was a pause. A long pause.

"Perhaps she doesn't know," said Pete.

"It may not be easy finding your own body," I pointed out.

"I never have any trouble," he said.

HONK! HONK! HONK! HONK! HONK! HONK!

"I think she's found herself," Angie said.

The excited honking had come from the far end of the yard, the out-of-sight part of the L-shape. We jumped over Mom's terrific new rock garden, brushing the flowers and stuff with our heels, and ran around the corner. I was getting this sinking feeling.

"Say it again, old goose," Pete said. "We're not psychic."

HONK!

The sinking feeling hit my sneakers. My feet twitched. A Latin American rhythm started to jerk through me. I sniffed one of the perfect little pink flowers, dancing. Here of all places. Aunt Hetty's body was sitting right under the only thing my dad ever planted that lived. His pride and joy. The Rodadoodah bush.

13

After we laid the Rodadoodah bush on the grass beside its hole, we dug on with a spade and a couple of trowels from the shed. We all saw it at once. The sack that contained the body. We were pretty pleased with ourselves until we realized that none of us wanted to actually touch it.

"Whaddaya say we cover it up again?"

"Mm. Good plan."

"Could do it tomorrow."

"Or the day after."

"Even better."

But like the good brave Musketeers we were, we reached in and took hold of the sack, shuddered a bit, and tugged. It didn't want to come up, but we got it out eventually and stood wiping our hands on our jeans in case they'd touched worms or something else too disgusting to think about.

"Go on then," Pete said. "Open it."

"No, you," I said, breaking into a silent tap dance on the turf.

"Your yard, your goose."

"Be my guest."

"Oh—men!" Angie said, and elbowed us aside.

She untied the sack and spread it open. We looked in. It was not a pretty sight. Even Hetty sounded affected by it.

SSSSSSssssssssssssSSSSSSSsss

Then the smell hit us. You could almost see it rising. Three dirt-stained hands slapped over three noses, passing the stain on. Angie closed the sack.

"Better put the bush back," I said, taking the lead in a fox-trot.

It wasn't till the Rodadoodah was back in its hole that I stopped dancing and just sagged for a while. Without the sack down there below it, the bush was about half its former height.*

---

*A couple of days later I found Dad walking around it, muttering, "I don't get it, I don't get it, I followed all the instructions. I even watered it once." By then it wasn't just a dwarf Rodadoodah, it was a dead dwarf Rodadoodah, without a single dinky little pink flower to its name.

Still, there was nothing we could do about it. "Now," I said, "the shopping center."

Pete pulled a face. "Are you out of your skull? Where was it your mother just went?"

"Oh yeah," I said.

"Besides," said Angie. "Broad daylight when everything's still open might not be a good idea. And we haven't decided where to rebury her yet."

"I thought we said where the farmhouse used to be."

"They built the main square over the farmhouse," Pete said. "We can't dig up the main square, someone might notice."

"It's not all paved over. What we have to work out is where one of the rooms was, and if it's the sort of spot you can leave dead geese in, we're in business."

"Wait a minute," Angie said. "There's this big old tree in the square, with railings around it. Used to be in Brooky's front yard."

"I don't remember a tree with railings in Brooky's front yard," Pete said.

"It didn't have railings then, dummy," said Ange.

"Yeah, that's right," I said. "The biggest branch hung right over the house. So all we have to do is see what's under the branch now."

"What if it's solid concrete?" Pete said.

"Then we have a problem."

"Hetty's very quiet," Angie said.

"Maybe something to do with the fact that she's dead?" said Pete.

"I mean poltergoose Hetty."

"Probably in shock," I said. "Wouldn't you be if you came across your bones and stuff in an old sack?"

"Hetty?" Angie called softly. "Aunt Hetty, you there?"

Not a sound. Nothing.

"Perhaps she's cleared off now that we've found her body," Pete said. "Perhaps we can just chuck it over a hedge and go and watch TV."

SSSSSSsssssssssssssSSSSSSsss

"Or maybe not."

There were several hours to kill before the shopping center closed, so we had to hide the sack. There was only one place we could think of.

"Look, Hetty," I said to the empty air, "don't get your feathers in a twist or anything, we'll take you out later, I promise. It's just to keep you safe, all right?"

The good thing about the trash can was that it had been emptied that morning. It still whiffed a bit (though it was pretty sweet compared to the open sack) but it did the job. It must have been okay with Aunt Hetty anyway, because we didn't hear a peep out of her as we dropped the sack containing her sad old feathers and bones in the can.

14

It was eight o'clock, the time we'd arranged to meet by the trash can. Pete and Angie were late. When they finally turned up Angie said it was because Pete kept finding other things he'd rather do than spend the evening with a dead goose. We flipped open the can.

"Holy underpants!"

"It's a conspiracy!"

"Unbeli*eeeee*vable!"

Mom must have been saving all the trash till the can was emptied, because it was now three-quarters full of used paper towels, soggy wrappers, and old chili. And all of it on top of the Hetty sack.

"We could always wheel it to the mall," I suggested.

"People might wonder what three kids are doing pushing a trash can around," Angie said. "And we'd still have to get the sack out when we got there."

"I'm not going in there," Pete said. "Here *or* at the mall."

Angie called him a name I'd never heard before and took charge for the second time that day, or maybe the third. And my dad says women are the weaker sex!

"Jiggy, go and fetch some rubber gloves from the kitchen."

"Rubber gloves? There's only the dishwashing gloves, and my mom's wearing those."

"Well, I want *something* over my hands," she said. "Hey, I know. Hankies."

"Hankies?" said Pete and I together.

The boss snapped her fingers. "Come on, come on."

We fished out our hankies. Angie curled her lip.

"Forget it. I'll risk the Black Death. Now tilt the can. Tilt it right over."

We tilted the can until it was almost flat on the ground and most of the stuff inside had tumbled out. We pulled faces, grunted, said things like "Eeeeerrrgg," and then Ange—amazing Ange—reached in bare-handed, grabbed the sack, and pulled.

It didn't budge.

"You too," she ordered.

"Not me," Pete said.

She screwed her eyes up at him. "Sorry? Didn't quite catch that."

He took a corner of the sack in a finger and thumb. So did I.

"Get *ahold* of it!" Angie said fiercely.

We got ahold of it. A couple of hearty tugs and the sack was out, and we sat there covered in trash. Most of the garbage was loose stuff, easily shaken off, but the beans and cat litter and soggy cereal seemed to get into everything, and I don't just mean clothes.

"You stink," said Pete to me.

"It's my dad's new deodorant, Trash Can for Men."

The next problem was getting all the stuff back in, which for some strange reason was even less fun than getting it out. When we'd done that, we ran back shuddering to the backyard for some clumps of grass to wipe ourselves down. (That's how we came to have green stains all over us as well as the rest.) When we got back to the sack we found two cats sniffing at it with interest.

"Shoo!"

"Scat!"

"Vamoose!"

Then, all set, we strolled off in the direction of the shops, whistling different tunes, hoping that three kids pulling a sack looked normal. Most people ignored us, but a few grinned in that superior way adults do when they're saying to one another: "Kids—what will they think of next?"

Hey. If only they knew.

As expected, the shopping center was deserted by the time we got there. (It's always deserted from about fifteen minutes after the shops close till about nine when the muggers climb out of bed and the drunks start rolling up to dance with the lampposts.) There wasn't even anyone snoozing in the flower beds yet. All just about perfect, in fact, for disposing of dead geese.

Until Pete spotted the downside. "Major snag," he said.

I thumped him. But then I saw what he meant. "*Now* whaddawedo?"

We'd forgotten the new security cameras. We stood in a doorway with our sack of goose, watching two of them pan for vandals. We would have watched all four, but a couple of them weren't moving. They'd been vandalized.

"There's the tree with the railings," Angie said.

"Glad you pointed it out, Ange," I said. "Nearly missed it there."

The big old tree that had once grown wild and free in Mr. Brook's front yard now stood imprisoned in a neat little railing in the middle of the square. Everything else around the tree might have changed, but you couldn't mistake the enormous branch that used to hang over the house. It still hung there, over the place we had to put Hetty so she could R.I.P. and stop pestering me.

The Brook Farm Shopping Center Public Rest Rooms.

"The first person to say anything about feeling a bit flushed," I said, "is in big trouble."

"Come on," Angie said. "Let's case the joint."

"Hold on," Pete said. "One of the cameras is turning this way."

We waited while the camera panned slowly by, then made a run for the bathrooms.

We waited while the camera panned the other way, then ran back for the sack.

"Whew," said Pete when we were at the bathrooms again.

I couldn't have expressed it better myself. This was

nerve-racking stuff. My feet had started moving in small rhythmic circles, my hips were swaying, fingers clicking.

There were two doors to the block of toilets beneath the branch. One of them had the word *Ladies* over it. The other had the word *Gets,* because someone had stolen the "n." The Gets was boarded up, probably because the graffiti-covered door on the other side of the boards hung on only one hinge.

"This one's okay," Angie whispered from the next doorway.

We joined her, dragging the sack between us. There were no boards over the other door, it hung on both hinges at once, and it hadn't been locked up for the day yet. Angie went in. The door closed behind her.

Pete and I looked at each other. Then we looked at the door. Then we looked at each other again. Then we looked at Angie, who'd just opened the door to look out at us.

"What are you waiting for, a personal invitation?"

"We can't go in there," Pete said.

"It's only a rest room," said Ange.

"It's a *Ladies* rest room," I reminded her.

"So?"

"Well, we're not ladies."

"Camera's coming," Pete said.

We pushed past Angie. The door closed behind us. Pete Garrett and Jiggy McCue were in the Brook Farm Shopping Center Ladies Rest Room.

"I'll never live this down," said Pete.

"Nor will I," I said.

"I won't tell if you don't," he said.

"Deal," I said. We slapped hands, then wiped them on our jeans.

Then it hit us. The smell. And we thought dead goose in an old sack was bad?

"Phwah!" Pete said, palming his nose into his skull.

I did likewise. "No wonder there's a hole in the ozone layer."

"Remind me to inspect the Gets sometime," Angie muttered.

Pete and I looked around. We didn't like to, but it went with the job. What we saw on the walls shocked us to the core.

"I didn't know you got stuff like this in the Ladies Room," Pete marveled. "I thought only fellas wrote this sort of thing."

"The drawings aren't bad," I said.

"When you two have stopped admiring the artwork," Angie said, "we have to decide where to put Hetty's bones."

"No problem," said Pete.

He kicked one of the three stalls open and bowed like a magician expecting applause. He didn't get any.

"No," I said. "Not there. It'd be disrespectful."

"She's a goose. She'll probably think it's an honor to be flushed into the main drainage system."

"You there, Hetty?" I said through the filthy hankie that was now over my face. "How would you feel about floating out to sea, Het? You wouldn't be alone."

If she was in there with us she was too choked with emotion to reply. Either that or she'd stayed outside because she couldn't stand the smell.

"We'd have to take her apart bone by bone to get her down there," Angie said. "Her beak would probably get stuck around the bend too. No, we'll have to think of something else."

"This is a public rest room," Pete said. "Public rest rooms have two things. They have sinks and they have toilets. If you want to get rid of anything here, that's the choice."

"There might be one other place," I said, strolling

over to the sinks. There were three of them, to match the stalls. Below the middle one was the drain that all the gungy washing water slopped into. There was an iron grille over the drain. The grille had this nice flowery pattern riddled with holes. I tapped it with my foot.

"It's not much bigger than the toilet," Pete said.

"Big enough, though," I said. "Wouldn't have to pull her apart to get her down there, just get her to breathe in a bit."

"See if you can get the cover off," Angie said.

My eyes raced over the floor I'd have to kneel on to do that small thing. It wasn't all that clean, but for the first time I was glad this was the Ladies Room rather than the Gets. In the Gets, the customers take aim at the wall, close their eyes, and spray everything they can't see, including their feet, neighboring pants, and the ceiling. After a day's zipper action in the Gets, the floor is a swamp. At least this one was dry. I got down on it and inspected the drain cover.

"Anybody got a screwdriver?"

"Sure," Pete said. "I always carry a screwdriver. Would you like my hammer and nails while you're at it? My electric sander? My Black and Decker drill?"

Angie leaned down. "What do you want a screw-driver for? No screws."

"No, but I have to get something under the grille to pull it up, and a screwdriver would probably do it."

"Use your fingers."

"Use *your* fingers," I said. "Mine are reserved for ear-wax duty."

"Wimp," she said, and yanked me away from the drain. She dropped to her knees and hooked her fingers into the grille. I watched, filled with admiration and disgust.

Pete wandered over to the door for a lung of fresh air. Angie and I were still crouched over the drain when I heard him say: "What do you call a man in an envelope?"

"What are you talking about?" I said.

"It's a joke. What do you call a man in an envelope?"

"I don't know. Don't care."

"Bill," he said. No one laughed. Then he said: "Some-one's coming."

"Is this another joke?"

"No. Someone's coming."

"Who?"

"How would I know, she's not carrying a sign with

her name on it. But she looks like she's coming here. Two guesses what for."

There was a clang followed by a yelp as Angie jumped up and banged her head on the sink. She bolted past me into one of the stalls and slammed the door. Pete bolted past me into another stall and slammed the door. I bolted past me into the third stall and slammed the door. I would have bolted the door too, but the bolt had been stolen. I parked my rear on the seat and slapped my soles on the door.

"Who's got the sack?" Angie's voice, muffled by distance and stall walls.

"Not me," said Pete, also muffled but not quite as much.

"It's still out there," I informed them.

There was a small pause. We could hear footsteps now, tappy-tap-tapping in the square.

"Maybe she'll miss it," said Angie.

"Maybe she won't," said Pete.

Another small pause. The tappy-taps were closing in. Angie said: "Something just occurred to me. There are three stalls, and they're all full, two of them with boys."

"Well?" I said.

"Well, if that woman wants to use one she's going to be disappointed."

"Good," Pete said, "then she'll shove off."

"No, she won't. No one would use this place unless they were desperate. She'll cross her legs and wait for an empty stall."

"She'll have a long wait."

"We can't stay in here forever."

"Oh, I don't know," said Pete.

"Pete," I said. "Move over, I'm coming in."

I separated my feet from the door, intending to make a fast switch to his stall and jostle for seat space, but just as I opened up, the lady came in. I froze.

"Hi. Nice evening."

She also froze. "This is the Ladies Room," she said.

"I know," I said. "I was just looking for my sack. Ah, there it is."

I grabbed the Hetty sack and dragged it past her, smiling hard.

16

Out in the square I hid behind the tree in the railings to fool the cameras. The seconds ticked by. I counted them into minutes. One minute, two minutes, three minutes, four. At the stroke of five and a quarter the woman came out and waltzed off around the corner of the supermarket. I lugged Hetty back into the Ladies Room.

"It's all right, she's gone," I said to the two closed stalls.

"Whew!" said Angie.

Her door opened. So did Pete's. He peered out. All the color had drained from his face. "That was the most horrible experience of my life," he said.

"I need help," said Angie, holding up her hand. It was wearing the drain cover. Her fingers were like macramé.

"Leave it to me, Ange," I said, and bent her fingers back.

She screamed.

I bent them the other way.

She screamed again, but the cover was off.

We set to work.

It wasn't much easier forcing the sack of Hetty remains down that little drain than it had been getting it up out of the Rodadoodah hole, but we did it. That is, Angie did it, with me pushing at her shoulders and her telling me to stop. Pete watched the door. Every now and then he watched the square outside too. No one else came.

I felt quite sad when Hetty and her sack were squashed tight into the drain and Angie had banged the grille back into place. I mean, we'd been close in our way. I still had the dents in my behind to prove it. But we'd done it. Laid her to rest in the drain of her dreams. And I was a free man again.

When we left the shopping center, I crossed the road to the sparkling new houses of the Brook Farm Estate, and Pete and Angie shunted off toward the Old Town and Borderline Way, where half the streetlights had been successfully used for target practice and cars lived on bricks.

"Thanks, gang," I called merrily as we waved good-bye.

"It was a real pleasure," said Pete. "Next time use a neighbor."

Before I slipped out of the house earlier without telling Mom and Dad, I thought of leaving a compilation CD playing in my room, set on "Repeat" so it would never finish and they'd think I was still up there. I didn't in the end because I decided that no one would be stupid enough to fall for that one. So the house was silent apart from the TV in the living room as I tiptoed upstairs and opened the door of my room.

Mom and Dad were sitting on the bed, waiting for me. My hand trembled on the doorknob. They looked a little tense.

"We were just going to call the cops," Dad said.

"The cops?" I said, my recent life somersaulting past my eyes.

"Where have you been?" said Mom.

"To the bathroom. I went to the bathroom."

"No, you didn't. We looked in both bathrooms."

"Hey," I said, "isn't it cool to be able to say that? Couldn't have said that in the old days, at good old Borderline Way."

"I said where have you *been,* Jiggy?" Mom repeated, a little coldly, I thought.

"Why? Did I miss something?"

Dad chipped in. "Cut the smart talk, Jig. Your mom's been worried half out of her tree. And before you go to the trouble of inventing something else I called Oliver to see if you'd sneaked off somewhere with Angie and Pete."

"What did he say?"

"He said you hadn't, they've been upstairs all evening playing the same boring record over and over."

"Enough of this," Mom said. She leaned forward, gritted her teeth, spoke in italics. *"Where—have—you—been?"*

I thought furiously. "I went for a walk," I said. "Around the estate. To see how the gardens are coming along, count the gnomes—you know."

"Jiggy, I've told you before, I do not want you wandering the streets at night. The sort of people that hang around out there, it's simply not safe."

"You've got to let me out sometime," I said.

"Yes well, let's wait till you stop reading comics, shall we?"

"I still read comics," Dad said.

"Mel, that sort of remark doesn't help at all," Mom said. "Look at him, he's relaxed again."

"Sorry. Not much good at the heavy parent stuff."

He got up to leave. He was about to pass me when his nostrils shot out like a mad horse's.

"Ever heard of showers, Jig?"

I put my fingers to my chin. "Hmm, that's a tough one."

"And the state of you, what have you been *doing*?"

"I went out like this."

"You deal with him," he said to Mom, and left the room.

When he'd gone, Mom said "Jiggy" in a much gentler voice and reached a hand out for me.

I took it, wondering if I should tell her to get a typhoid shot from the doc afterward.

"Yes, Mom?"

She pulled me closer. Her nostrils flared too, but she was too much of a gentleman to shudder. She sat me down beside her.

"Jiggy," she said again.

"Still here," I said.

"Promise me you won't do anything like that again."

"What, go out? You mean not even to school? Can I have that in writing?"

"You know what I'm talking about." Her eyes went all big and soft, and she added: "You're all we've got, you know."

"Well, that's not quite true," I said. "You've got the car, the TV, the washing machine. And don't forget your curling iron."

She threw my hand away, probably realizing it was contaminated, and stood up. She seemed upset.

"There's no point in even *trying* to talk to you, is there? Well, pay attention to this. I want you out of those things right this minute, you hear me? You will then go and have a good wash—and I mean *good* wash—and go straight to bed. I don't want to see hide nor hair of you till tomorrow morning, when I expect a full apology for worrying me sick. Do I make myself clear?"

"Yes, Mom."

She went. I leaned back on the bed. Suddenly I felt tired. Very, very tired. All I wanted was to get in there under the comforter and not wake up till the end of the week when school was over. Still, I had the satisfaction of knowing that my poltergoose troubles were over. Never again would I see Aunt Hetty's shadow on my wall. Never again see rocking horses butchered before my eyes, or gorillas fall off hooks, or lights torn from ceilings. Never again would I be chased downstairs by a beak.

There was probably a happy grin on my face as my bed suddenly tipped up, flew across the room, and hit the opposite wall with me still on it. As the bed rocked back and I rolled onto the floor with a bowl of white plastic flowers in my hands, an insane honking, like no honking I ever heard before, filled the room.

But that wasn't all. Not quite. Suddenly these colossal great lumps of soft stuff were hailing down from the ceiling.

Goose droppings from hell.

And then my mother and father were rushing back in, screaming my name and threatening to ground me for the rest of my life if I didn't stop this outrageous, this childish, this totally unacceptable behavior. We didn't discuss the goose droppings. I don't think they wanted to know, somehow.

17

So Hetty didn't care for life after death in a public drain, and she wasn't going to leave me in peace till we found her some place more to her liking.

"Pity she didn't mention it before," Angie said when I told her and Pete at school the next day.

"And where else are we supposed to put her?" Pete said.

"I don't know, but it has to be soon, like tonight. At breakfast my dad was looking through the Yellow Pages for straitjacket suppliers."

"We can't do anything tonight. Your parents' wacky housewarming dinner thing."

"If we don't do it tonight," I said, "Hetty might lose her goosey cool and completely destroy the wacky housewarming dinner thing, along with what's left of my sanity."

"Jiggy's right," said Angie. "We have to act fast."

We arranged to meet by the shopping center at eight to haul Hetty out of the Ladies Room and back to my place. Thought we might stick her under the dwarf Rodadoodah again until we figured out what to do next. But then Angie called and told me to bring a spade.

"What do we want a spade for?" I asked. "We can pull her out."

"It's for putting her where she ought to be."

"We don't know where she ought to be."

"I do," she said. "I went back to the shopping center after school and realized where we went wrong. Tell you later. Eight o'clock, with spade."

At ten to eight, all dressed up in the clothes my mother laid out specially to make me feel really stupid (creases down the front of my jeans and all), I stuck my head around the kitchen door. Mom was bending over the stove like a witch, stirring something, and Dad was sitting on a stool looking at the pictures in the free local paper he never reads.

"Mom, what time's this dinner thing?"

"I told Aud and Oliver eight, eight-thirty."

"What does that mean?"

"Which means we sit down to eat on the dot of nine forty-three," Dad muttered from behind the paper.

"So I've got . . . how long exactly?"

"One hour," said Mom.

"And a half," said Dad. "At least."

"Where do you think you're going anyway?" Mom asked, looking up from her stirring.

"Meeting Pete and Angie. We'll have a little chat, then they'll come back with me."

"Then you can go upstairs and put a sweater on. I don't want you getting that clean shirt dirty."

"I won't get it dirty."

"Don't argue or I'll remember what I said last night about you not going out again as long as you live."

I tore all my hair out, jumped on it, and ran back to my room. I grabbed the first woolly thing in my drawer, stuck my head through it, and hopped down again, six stairs at a time.

Out in the yard, I whipped a spade from the shed.

"You there, Hetty?" I said.

SSSSss

"Come on then, race you! And no beaking!"

I legged it for the shopping center, accompanied by

the occasional feathery flap. Like last time, the square was deserted and quiet. Angie and Pete were already there, standing well back from the cameras. Like me, they were in their best duds. They too had embarrassing creases down their jeans.

The first thing Angie said when I jogged into view wasn't, as you might expect, "Hi, Jig, glad you could make it, see you got the spade, you're my hero." No, it was: "Jiggy McCue, are you out of your pathetic excuse for a *mind*?"

"Naturally, only place to be," I zapped back. "Why do you ask?"

"The sweater?" she said wearily.

I looked down at my sweater from on high. It was the one my grandma had knitted with her own wrinkly little hands. The blue one with JIGGY screaming across the front in luminous orange letters as big as an elephant's behind. My mother had asked me to remove it from under my bed, and when I didn't she must have rescued it and put it where I couldn't miss it—where I *hadn't* missed it.

I heard a small gasping sound near my feet. Pete's knees had given way and he was folded up on the ground in silent hysterics. Angie and I stood looking at the sky while he gagged down there for another minute, then he got up, tears streaming down his neck. He couldn't look at me.

The Ladies Room sat across the square, waiting for us. "Anyone in there?" I said.

"Not unless they've got a problem," Angie said. "We've been here ten minutes. Come on, and mind those cameras—specially you, cement-head."

We loaded our feet and fired them across the square. It wasn't till we reached the Ladies Room and were halfway through the door that we noticed dirty water splashing up our nice clean jeans. This took our attention away from the smell of the place, but we may have forgotten to be grateful as we slithered to a halt at the sinks. From the look of it, the water was bubbling out of the drain underneath instead of gurgling gently into it.

"Must be blocked up with something," Pete said, wading right back to the door.

"I'm not putting my hand down there this time," Angie said.

"Come on, Ange," I said. "You're so good at it."

"Well, it's about time someone *else* got good at it then, isn't it? Like you."

"But I'll get all wet," I said. "Wetter."

"That's your brain leaking all over that stupid sweater. Get down there."

She was in that dangerous mood again. I rolled up my woolly hand-knitted sleeves, plunged a neatly creased knee into the canal that swirled around us, and closed my eyes in misery.

"What's it feel like?" Pete said, leaning in the door on his toes.

"Shut up," I said.

The drain cover was all slimy, like seaweed or poached slugs. My stomach turned over as I stuck my fingers in. I tugged. The grille didn't budge. I tugged again. Slight movement. I put everything I had into it— and shot backward, full length, into the water, fingers neatly interwoven with the pretty iron pattern.

"You wanna be careful," Pete said from the door. "Spoil your nice party clothes."

"Angie," I said, splashing to my feet, "untie my fingers, will you? I want to put them in Pete's eyes."

"Get away from me," she said. "I'm as wet as I'm going to get."

"*You're* wet?" I said. "Compared to me you're the Sahara Desert!"

"Do you know what 'sahara' means in Arabic?" Pete said. "*Desert.* It means *desert.* True. Read it on a cereal box the other day. So when we say 'Sahara Desert' what we're really saying is 'Desert Desert.' How about that?"

"I'm gonna kill him," I said to Angie.

Angie pulled herself together and unlaced my fingers. I dropped the grille into the water. It sank without trace.

"Now the sack," she said. "Pete, get in here."

"No chance," said Pete.

"PETE!"

He splashed in, scowling. "This is all your fault, McCue. You and that stupid goose of yours."

SSSSSSssssssssssssSSSSSSSsss

"You still here?" he said.

I stood back while Angie guided Pete's hands into the drain and he grabbed the sack, whimpering.

"Well, don't just kneel there," she said to him. "Pull it out."

"What do you think I'm trying to do, pluck its feathers one by one?"

But then he pulled a bit harder, and pulled again, and once more, and then—

SPLASH!

Over he went, on his back, the sack on top of him. "Well done, Pete." I grabbed the sack before it floated away. Pete just lay there, spluttering and thrashing around.

Angie and I went to the door. "People," she said, looking out.

There were two of them, a couple, plus a silly little dog, wasting their lives looking in a closed shop window. In a minute they wandered off, but not before the dog had cocked his leg at the window to show what he thought of the display.

"To the tree!" Angie said when their heels had clicked away to nothing.

Dodging the two roving lenses, we dragged the sack across the square, leaving a wet sacky trail for Pete to follow when he stopped doing the backstroke in the Ladies Room.

"Hetty?" I said when we got to the tree. "Are you with us or back there paddling around with Pete?"

S S S S ss s s

"Sounds a bit beaked off," said Angie.

"She's not the only one. So where did we go wrong yesterday?"

"We were facing the wrong way."

"No, no, can't have been," I said. "That branch definitely hung over the house, I remember it vividly."

"You vividly remember the wrong branch. The one hanging over the bathrooms is not the one that hung over the farmhouse. Looks the same 'cause it's about the same size, same model, but it's not the one. They lopped off the branch we were looking for when they built the square around the tree to show how much they care about nature."

"How do you know which one got lopped?"

"Remember the last time we worked for old Brooky, when we went up to the house to plead for our wages? His goose—Hetty, as we now know—came at us like we were Jehovah's Witnesses or something. Half terrified us."

"More than half," I said.

"And when she flew at us I fell over this great root."

"What great root?"

"This great root."

We looked at the great root at the base of the tree. Most of it was inside the railings, but there was a little warning sign near the part they couldn't get in. The little warning sign said: WATCH OUT FOR THE ROOT.

"And this root," Angie said, "pointed to the very room where Mr. Brook and Hetty played Scrabble in their pajamas on chilly nights."

"And now it's pointing at a flower bed. Which is why you wanted me to bring the spade."

"Right. But it's a bit exposed, so we'll have to watch those cameras. Dash out, dig, dash for cover when a camera comes, dash out, dig, dash for cover when a cam—"

"What's Pete up to?" I said.

Pete had finally quit the Ladies Room and was sauntering across the square like a tourist whose luggage has gone to the Bahamas without him. Wet footprints followed him. The cameras took turns sweeping across him. We shouted at him to cover his face, and get a move on before he was broadcast to the entire world by satellite.

"I'm past caring!" he shouted back.

Angie had already told Pete her idea, so she didn't need to repeat it when he eventually joined us in hiding.

"But we don't know for certain that Hetty wants to be buried in a flower bed," I said. "I mean she hasn't exactly *said*, has she."

"So ask her," said Ange.

"Hetty," I said to a nearby patch of nothing, "now I

want you to think carefully before you answer, because I don't want you wrecking my reputation at *The Dorks* again. Or my room. See that flower bed over there? That's where your old living room was. Now what I want you to tell us is: do you . . . want us . . . to bury . . . your remains . . . *there*?"

S S S S s s s s s

"Is that a yes or a no?" Angie whispered.

"Was that a yes or a no, Hetty?"

S S S S S S S s s s s S S s s s s S

"Any questions?" I said to the others.

There were no questions, even from Pete, but that could be because he was too depressed to speak.

18

After making sure that the entire police department hadn't suddenly turned out to watch us (and that the cameras were looking the other way), Angie and I rushed to the flower bed. Since I had the spade, it was me who took first dig.

"Camera's coming," Angie said after two strokes.

We trotted back to the tree, where we'd left the sack with Pete, who seemed quite happy to spend his life there, dripping.

"Come on, Pete," I said. "One for all and all for lunch?"

"I'm not happy," he said. "I'm wet and I'm uncomfortable and the creases have fallen out of my jeans."

"You *like* creases in your jeans?"

"Doesn't everyone?"

"Camera's gone," said Ange.

I dashed out again, with her riding my heels. "Pete!" I hissed.

He drifted after us, stood wringing out his pockets and mumbling.

"Whew," I said. "Hot work."

"You've dug three inches," said Ange.

"Ground's hard."

"Pete, you take a turn."

Pete took the spade and turned it over a couple of times as if he'd never seen one before.

"Camera's coming," I said.

Pete threw the spade in the air and ran for cover like a madman. We followed, not quite as frantically. Those cameras are not fast swivelers.

"I have an idea," Angie said under the tree.

Pete groaned. "Just what we need, another idea."

"It's this. You don't dig, Pete, you just stand here and tell us what the cameras are doing."

"I like it," said Pete, cheering up immediately. "Camera's gone."

Angie and I dashed out. I started digging again. She snatched the spade from me—"Give me that!"—and did practically the whole job herself between runs. She didn't hang around either, just got on with it, no hassle, no complaints, no sweat—even under the arms so far as I could tell. When the hole was big enough we dropped the sack in and covered it over in double-quick time.

"What about flowers?" Angie said. "She ought to have flowers."

"She's got flowers," said Pete, who was getting it together again at last and running out and back with us. "She's in a bed of them."

"Yeah, but look at the state of it."

We looked at the state of the flower bed. It wasn't as colorful as it should have been, being as there weren't many flowers in it. We took in the other flower beds around the square. Ditto. It was flower-pinching season, and they were a little low on stock.

"Let's gather some up," Angie said.

We raided the other flower beds and replanted a fair selection over Hetty's grave between camera swivels.

"Snag," said Pete, right back in form now.

"Must you keep *saying* that?" I growled.

"Yes, but look. There are so many flowers over Hetty now, and so few everywhere else, that someone's bound to wonder what's down there."

I hated to admit it, but he was right. So we took a lot of the flowers out again and—dodging the cameras—

re-replanted them all over the place so no one would get suspicious.

When we'd finished, I said: "Shouldn't we say something?"

"How about 'Let's get outta here'?" said Pete.

"No, I mean some sort of . . . prayer or something."

"I've been saying prayers ever since we arrived."

"For Aunt Hetty."

"A prayer for a goose?" he said. "Gimme a break."

"Well, not a prayer exactly, just a few words. As a way of saying good-bye."

"I think 'Good-bye, Hetty' says it all."

"No, Jiggy has a point," said Angie. "This is a big moment in her life after all."

"In her *life?*" said Pete.

"Camera coming," I said.

We ran for cover. While we waited for the camera to move off, I asked if anyone had anything to write with.

"I've got a gel pen," Angie said.

I took the pen. "Any paper?"

"Not this side of the Ladies Room," said Ange.

"Camera's going," said Pete.

"Hang on, I'm going to write something for Hetty. Turn around, Pete."

"What for?"

"Just do it." I spread my snot-stiffened hankie across his back and started to write. I didn't let them see till I'd finished.

"That's not right," Pete said then.

"I know it's not *right*, I've adapted it for the occasion."

"It doesn't *fit* the occasion."

"Well, it's short notice; you got any better ideas?"

He hadn't. Nor had Angie. "It'll have to do," she said. "Hang around here much longer and we'll be released on DVD, with a commentary and theme song."

We went back to the flower bed, where we gathered in a solemn row of three. I held up my hankie, and we read my immortal lines, which I'd done a fair job of arranging around the hard little black bits, I thought.

> *"Hey diddle-diddle*
> *The cat did a piddle*
> *A cowpat fell off the moon*
> *The little dog barked to see such fun*
> *And the goose flew away too soon."*

And then the most amazing thing happened. Just as we finished my farewell to Aunt Hetty, there was this incredible noise from overhead. Naturally we looked up. And saw a flock of geese flying across the sky in this great V-shape.

"Now that," Pete said, "is what I call a coincidence."

As they flew, the geese flapped their wings so slowly you wondered how they stayed up there. Their necks were stretched right out, and their beaks made this sound, like a cross between a pack of hounds chasing a fox and a bunch of cracked old bells. I think I said, "Wow."

"Twenty-four," Angie breathed in my ear.

"Uh?"

"There's twenty-four of them. Eleven on one side, twelve on the other, plus the one in front making the point of the V. Twenty-four."

HONK!

We grabbed hold of one another. That was one loud honk. And close. "Hetty . . ." one of us said, or perhaps it was all of us.

HONK!

Not quite so loud this time, and up a bit. Then there it was again.

HONK!

And again, and again, and again. And each time invisible Hetty honked she did it a bit farther away, a bit higher up the sky.

HONK! HONK!

HONK!
HONK!

"Awesome," Pete murmured.

The shadow of a flying goose had appeared, very high up, approaching the V-shaped formation.

"Go on, girl," I said. "Go on, you can do it."

"Twenty-five!" Angie laughed as Hetty clicked into place at the tail end of the shorter line.

"Awesome," said Pete again.

"Awesome," said Angie.

"Awesome," said I, and hoisted the spade to wave good-bye to the dear old goose.

19

As we approached the back gate, we heard music. Well, music. Sad Golden Oldie stuff so ancient that Noah danced to it with a hippo in the Ark. We opened the gate. I hid the spade. We went around the L-shape. Audrey Mint and Oliver Garrett and Dad were on the patio admiring Mom's rock garden. Dad obviously hadn't been to look at the Rodadoodah lately because he was smiling. All three of them were in their best clothes and all clean and shiny. Unlike us. They noticed this. So did Mom when she trotted out of the house five seconds later.

"Jiggy! I don't believe what I'm seeing!"

I held my hands up. I'd had it with explanations.

"Well, you can just go right upstairs this minute and wash. All of you. And you," she said, glaring at me in particular, "can change out of those *filthy* things."

"I can't do that," I said. "Then I'd be the only neat one."

"He has a point, Peg," said Audrey. "Unless you think we should take the other two home to change too . . . ?"

Mom threw her bottom lip out. "The meal's almost ready."

"Oh, leave 'em be," Dad said. "They've looked worse."

Mom threw some daggers at him, but he ducked and she gave in.

"Very well, but give yourselves a *good* wash. And be sharp about it; we're eating in five minutes!"

We went upstairs. I ran along the landing and threw my bedroom door back. "Hetty?"

No answer. And the room felt different somehow. Gooseless. I could live with that.

"Gone!"

"Good riddance," Pete said. "I never *ever* want to see another goose, alive or dead."

"Me neither," said Ange.

We went to the bathroom, looked at the taps over the sink, decided it would be a shame to make the handles dirty, and went back to my room, where I finally found a use for Roger the gorilla, brushing off dirt and other grunge with his skinny arms. I had just dumped Grandma's sweater back under the bed when Mom called.

We went down, past the kitchen where the old dear was slaving away on her own. "Smells great, Mom," I said to cheer her up. "Hope it's burgers."

"It's not," she said, miserable as sin.

We went out to the backyard.

"You look very pleased with yourselves," Oliver said.

"That's 'cause we're young and have our whole lives ahead of us," Pete said, "and you're old and you've had yours."

Oliver gave him a nasty grin. "Obnoxious brat."

"Have you heard the news?" my dad said to us.

"What news?"

He glanced at Audrey and Oliver. "Can I tell them or do you want to?"

Oliver put his arm around Aud, still grinning. "Go ahead, Mel."

Pete clutched his head. "Oh no, they're gonna get *married.*"

A strangled sound came from Angie. "They can't do that. Then you and I would be related. Almost . . . brother and sister."

A dozen freckles jumped off Pete's nose. "You can't be best friends with your sister; it's impossible!"

Dad and Aud and Oliver had picked up on some of this and were chuckling like loons.

"No, no, no," Oliver said. "We wouldn't be stupid enough to get *married*."

Aud's grin twitched almost to nothing, She lurched away from him. "No, we'd never do something as stupid as *that*."

"Whew," said Pete and Angie, and slapped palms.

"They're going to buy a house on the estate," Dad said. "We're all going to be neighbors again!"

More freckles popped off Pete's nose. "You mean move? Move from Borderline Way?"

"Don't worry, Pete," Mom said as she came out from the kitchen again, "we know a behavioral psychologist who no longer has a picture over his chair. It's ready, everyone."

The Golden Oldies rubbed their hands together and stampeded into the house.

"It's no *so* bad on the estate," I said as we trailed after them. "Once you get used to the newness and all."

"Yeah, but I've lived on Borderline Way all my life," Pete said.

"So had I, but I made it out of there and survived—just."

"And we'll all be able to go to school together again," Angie said.

Pete grunted. "Better than getting related to each other, I s'pose."

"Million times better than *that*," said Ange.

We went into the house. The dining room looked great. Mom had really done a nice job there. Napkins in wooden rings and bright new silverware and place mats and dishes of veggies and sauces and stuff. No burgers. Dad was already in his place at one end of the table, and Audrey and Oliver sat on one side, with the three chairs opposite them meant for us. There was a bit of a scuffle while we jostled one another for the best seats. Angie got the middle one and smacked our arms till we stopped trying to get her out of it.

"All set, everyone?" Mom bawled from the kitchen.

"All set!" we bawled back.

She came in carrying this huge silver platter that I hadn't seen before, with this huge silver dome on it.

"What is it, Mom? Chicken? Turkey?"

"Wait and see."

She set the silver platter down in the middle of the table.

"Hope you all like this. Otherwise it's back to the can opener."

Six heads leaned forward, twelve nostrils twitching

in anticipation as Mom lifted the silver dome. And there it was, our housewarming dinner. Big, plump, steaming, and so tender-looking you could almost taste it already. Three adults slapped their lips and reached for their forks so they wouldn't have to waste any time when it was on their plates.

"Mom," I said nervously. "Mom, it's not . . . it's not a . . . ?"

"It's a goose," Mom said. "I don't think you've ever had roast goose befo— Jiggy?"

I'd jumped up. My chair had hit the wall behind me. *Smack*.

"What's with you?" Dad said.

Two more chairs hit the wall. *Smack. Smack.* Pete and Angie were also on their feet.

"Angie!"

"Pete, what the hell are you playing at?"

Hands over our mouths, skin the color of old broccoli, we broke all records for table-to-door sprinting, hoofed it along the hall, past the kitchen, through the back door. We made it outside only just in time. Threw ourselves gratefully onto my mother's terrific new rock garden.

"One for all and all for luuuuuunnnn . . ."

We almost got it out, almost but not quite. Got something else out instead. Mom didn't appreciate that. Nor did the others. You know the way parents stick together, gang up on you because they're bigger and fatter and give you an allowance. Mom said she'd never be able to look at that rock garden again without seeing the three of us sprawled across it heaving like there was no tomorrow. I felt the same, but for me it was one of those great moments. The Three Musketeers, side by side, us against the world. Pals, chums, buds to the bitter end.

20

Guess what. The local paper just came through the door, and right there on the front page there's a picture of this kid at the shopping center. He's got flowers on his shoulders and this lunatic grin on his face as he looks up, and because he's waving a spade in the air (which looks like a weapon the way he's holding it) you have to believe he's going to destroy something. And he's wearing this horrible sweater with a word as big as a bus on the chest. The word is JIGGY. The caption under the photo says:

THE BROOK FARM VANDAL.
DO YOU KNOW THIS BOY?

Hey. Some days you can't win, whatever you do.

JiGGY McCUE